CLAIRE BECKETT AND THE BLACK ORDER

CLAIRE BECKETT: PROTECTOR OF CRESCENT CITY

MOLLY CHASE

OPAL INK PUBLISHING

To Laramie,
For reading anything I write. Thank you.

ONE

The light outside my mother's cottage had already started to set, which meant I needed to head back into town. With a quick glance around the main room housing books, herbs, and all sorts of weapons, I once again felt close to my mother.

Sure, there were times I was still mad as hell at her for keeping me in the dark, but I had to remember Olivia Beckett, or Belinda Sanchez, as she was known here in Crescent City, had a reason for everything.

Like this cottage.

Ever since my long-lost cousin, Sloan, brought me here, I'd used every free minute I had searching through the books and documents, hoping I'd find the missing links to my past and, hopefully, my future. It was possible I had family out there, more than I'd had before coming to Crescent City.

My favorite find was a dictionary of *tvary*, the symbols I could see around dead bodies. It had taken a few weeks for me to go through it, highlighting the symbols I'd seen regularly at most crime scenes, but at the end was a small note penned in my mother's swoopy handwriting.

Claire,

If you're here, you've probably got a lot of questions. Hell, you've probably cursed me a few times for not telling you everything. Just know you're a great detective, like I always knew you would be, and that you'll solve all the puzzles about your background. Most of the answers are in this house. Use them to put things right, as I wasn't able to do.

I love you and know if there is an afterlife, I'll be there, doing my best to guide you. If not, I still have plenty of allies who are willing to do it in my place.

You can do this, Claire. Follow the trail and you'll understand. It was all for you.

Mom

I TEARED up a little every time I read it, but at least I finally had confirmation that she'd known I'd be here. When had she written the note? On one of her "work trips" she took every so often, in search of the latest news as a news correspondent for one of the local channels?

The rays of sun danced through the window, getting fainter as the sun sank behind the thick pine trees surrounding this place. Sonja, my well-loved but rusty car, didn't have headlights that shone well through the darkness, meaning now was the time to leave if I didn't want to run into something.

I grabbed the stack of books to my left, hoping I'd figure out more of what the symbols and words said within it. They weren't the same as the *tvary*, but something about them sparked the urge to learn more. To be honest, just about everything in this city did that to me. This was the first time since college the need to read non-fiction was burning within me. I hadn't realized how complacent I'd gotten at the 27th Precinct, but this city always kept me on my toes.

It had been about four weeks since we'd arrested Lyra and she was in a real jail, unlike Lee Vance, the shapeshifter we'd caught before her. The fact he'd managed to slip out of custody still sent chills through me. Nightmares of him tortured my sleep and the smallest thing would trigger the fear inside me. I just hoped I had backup the next time I faced him.

It didn't help settle my nerves that he was a shapeshifter and could literally be any person or creature I passed on a daily basis. Dr. Stringer, my work-mandated therapist, had been working through it with me over the past few weeks. Not the fact he was a shapeshifter, obviously, because I was pretty sure she was human, but all the normal human emotions that followed after trauma.

With the door of the cottage locked, I pressed two fingers together and drew in the air a three-symbol spell I'd learned from a spell book inside. The magic, what little it actually used, pulled over the house like a covering, the orange magic turning clear just moments after it had descended. Heath had something similar for the security system at his mansion, only his turned yellow. It made me wonder if it was because it was for a shifter, or just the type of magic used to conjure the protection spell.

Even now, several yards out, I glanced in the rearview mirror, seeing nothing where the cottage should be.

After a squeal, I couldn't contain my smile. I'd actually completed a spell from my mother's personal archives.

It had taken a lot of practice the past several times I'd left, the spell not always reaching the entirety of the cottage, but this one had gone off without a hitch, and on the first try this time. The exhilarated feeling made me want to pore over all the books in the house so I could learn all there was about my abilities.

I bumped along on the unpaved trail, the lack of shocks not

helping as I drove through the tree line. And then, a small sign stuck out of the ground I hadn't noticed before.

Lake Park Development.

This definitely didn't look like a lake, a park, or a development, but the sight of it made me grin wider than I had in weeks. It was one thing my mother definitely hadn't lied about. She'd always told me it was where she'd grown up, and being the naïve girl I'd been, I'd thought she meant South Boston.

Fifteen minutes after I'd left the cottage, I finally made it out to a road that led past the rest of the bruja lands and then the shifter region.

It was only around five, but the sun had already disappeared below the horizon, the last few offshoot rays keeping the sky as bright as possible.

Even though Sloan had warned me not to move into the house out in the woods, I was sorely tempted to sleep over from time to time. It took at least twenty minutes to get there from my apartment and no matter how many times I tried to race myself to get the time down, it was never below twenty.

I reached up to adjust the rearview mirror and noticed a car behind me. A shadow fell over the driver, shrouding the face in darkness and my heart pounded louder in my chest.

Lee wasn't here and I could defend myself.

It was like a chant I'd started a few weeks ago when the anxiety and nightmares about him coming for me turned for the worse.

I sucked in a breath, wishing I'd been able to understand how to unlock my lightning/electricity powers on my own.

The only thing I'd learned from my encounter with the psycho shapeshifter, Lee Vance, and the murdering vampire, Lyra Silver, was that when I got angry, I was able to throw out a bolt of electricity from my hand. But I still hadn't figured out to what level I had to descend to do it again.

I couldn't get mad enough on my own, even when combining all the secrets I'd learned over the past three months here in Crescent City. With my mother and my best friend, Tori, suffering death by a similar killer, finding out about the paranormal world and slowly learning I had powers had all caused anger to surge, but nothing to the point of summoning the electricity.

I'd tried to think of all the situations at once to produce the amount of anger and frustration I'd used on the previous two killers we'd arrested, without creating even a spark.

The car was still tailing me and I turned down a side street, curious what the driver would do. As I focused more on the form, I saw the silhouette of long hair and the body type, upper body anyway, wasn't the same as Lee's.

Breathe out. Count to five, like Dr. Stringer counseled me time and time again. I didn't need a full-on panic attack occurring while I was driving home. Tork, my partner, would never let me live it down. At one point, I'd thought Heath was like the head detective in the Paranormal PD, but it seemed he was fully invested in his role to guard me against unknown threats.

I thought about my mother's note again, wondering what had happened to require a protector for me. And did Nina have someone similar in her life? My half-sister had been dating the same guy for the past few years, but Tori had come into my life a year or so before my mother's death. I tried to think of the people Nina hung out with while she was in Boston, but no one stuck out as protector material.

Then again, Tori wasn't what I typically pictured as a bodyguard. She'd been average height and thin, but she could pack a punch when she needed to. It must've been the shifter side of her.

I'd have to ask Heath if anyone in his agency had been assigned to protect Nina.

I took several turns, grateful when the car behind me finally went the opposite direction, two blocks before my turn.

Paranoia didn't suit me.

I parked in my normal spot, lifting the five books I'd brought home to study more from the house, when I saw a pair of eyes in the darkness. They glowed a deep greenish/yellow, and I may have let out a slight cry as I dashed into the apartment building.

As much as I tried to mentally deny it, cats had begun to follow me no matter where I was. No, it wasn't a cat exodus from somewhere, but one or two would always be in my wake, sometimes leaving before another would take its place. Was that normal for most bruja?

Just another thing I needed to ask Sloan about.

Questions. I was full of them tonight and my detective brain demanded answers.

How was I supposed to contact Sloan, though?

Tork had mentioned the relationship between the Shadowmoon Bruja Coven and the rest of the paranormals in Crescent City had always been strained, meaning we, as the police, weren't allowed in uninvited. She'd told me I'd figure out how to find her, but there had been no magic spell that allowed secret passage onto coven lands.

And I didn't usually listen to what criminals said, but the way Lee had, "I would stay away from witches, Beckett," still rang in my mind. My mother stealing the Codex was an unforgivable act as far as he knew. I wasn't willing to test that rage.

Another thing I'd learned from the guys was the Shadowmoon Coven lands were locked down tighter than a jail. We should have just taken Lee there in the first place. Maybe they could have tortured him enough to ease the permanent knot in my stomach.

"How are you this evening, dear?" The words startled me,

as I was still thinking about the cats and why the bruja weren't willing to work with us.

My neighbor, Mrs. Samuels.

"Oh, hey. Sorry, I was lost in thought. I'm doing pretty well," I said, forcing a smile. The older woman was nice but I never knew what to talk to her about. I'd already become so accustomed to my life associating with paranormals that when people were human, I couldn't string more than a sentence together.

"I have some dinner for you," she said, turning and opening up her door.

"Oh, you don't have—" I stopped as she disappeared into her apartment. Did I walk into my own and shut the door? No, I could at least accept the gift.

A few seconds later, she walked out with hot pads on both sides of a casserole dish.

"I just never see you come up with groceries or take-out and I worry you aren't eating, dear."

That was odd. I didn't realize I was being watched in my own apartment building. Instead of giving a response, I reached forward to take the dish from her.

"No, dear. It's hot. Let me take it to the counter for you."

"Thanks," I said, trying to remember if I'd cleaned up after my long night of studying my mother's books the evening before. It was all I needed—to figure out how to explain books about symbols and paranormals to a human.

With the door open, I breathed out, grateful I'd put everything away.

"Thank you, Mrs. Samuels. You really didn't have to do that."

"This lasagna is a family recipe. And it should last you a couple of meals." She reached over and pinched the backside of my arm. "We need strong policewomen out there."

I nodded, trying to smile. It was such a strange compliment, but also gave me a watcher woman type vibe, and I knew I'd have to keep an eye out for her. Thankfully, she turned toward the door. I wasn't in the mood for more chit chat tonight.

"Just bring the dish back when you're done, dear," she said, stepping out into the hall. I thanked her and waited until she'd closed the door kitty-corner to me before I closed mine.

The food did smell delicious and it had been a while since I'd been grocery shopping to make anything edible. I didn't have to look in my cupboards to know there was only a box of stale cereal and several packets of hot chocolate. I'd given up trying to make my own coffee in the mornings, since the place around the corner from the precinct was heads and tails better than anything I could brew. Not having to pay rent and a sizeable raise once I made it to Crescent City allowed for that at least.

I was still paranoid I'd run into the woman who'd grown up with my mother, Adelaide, at the grocery store closest to me. She'd looked like she had lost her mind when I mentioned magic, and I didn't want to disturb the fragility of her conscience if she really was just a human.

I scooped out a portion of the lasagna onto a plate and sat at the bar, a book opened on the counter next to me. Taking a bite, I was pretty sure I was in heaven, because this was better than any lasagna I'd ever had, even from the North End in Boston. That was saying something.

What a difference Crescent City was to Boston. Even though I still loved that Dirty Water, I barely knew any of my neighbors there, both when I grew up and when I lived with Tori. Something about having an older person around to watch out for me was soothing when the rest of my days had been filled with the roller coaster ups and downs of wondering who I was and what I was. I would just have to make sure I remembered it though, in case anything nonhuman happened in the hallway.

My phone rang and I debated getting it from the entryway where I'd dropped it with my keys.

What if it was the precinct?

That was always my first thought, usually the reason guys didn't hang around for long. My career was full of thrills, never the same for longer than a few days to a few weeks. And the shot of adrenaline I got with each case we'd solved since I arrived kept pushing me toward the next.

The downside was we hadn't had many cases to solve in the past couple of weeks. Maybe everyone was taking a break for the holidays?

Find anything good today on your treasure hunt?

I tried to hold back a grin as I read Heath's text, but I couldn't. At least he wasn't here to see me react to it. We had a strange relationship where I tried to pretend he didn't affect me even though he was probably the hottest man I'd ever seen and he did everything he could to push my buttons.

I might have found a few things. I'm trying to go through some books but someone decided to interrupt my study session with a text.

It took five seconds to debate whether or not to send a smiley face with that one. I decided against it, wondering what he would say next.

Do you work tomorrow?

I raised an eyebrow, wondering what it had to do with all the information stored at my mom's little cottage in the woods. Sloan had forbidden me from bringing anyone else there, but he knew that was where I went more often now. Part of his bodyguard duties, I always assured myself.

Heath was the epitome of hot alpha leaders, and I was the quirky daughter of a bruja. What I'd inherited from my father was still a mystery, although my quick healing abilities were a sign I might be part shifter. I could handle it, as long as it wasn't something crazy.

Yes. I'll be at the precinct tomorrow.

Good. Get some sleep.

That was the response I got? Why did he even text me in the first place?

My pride took a nosedive and I turned off my phone, heading back to the comforts of the layered pasta and a book about spells. Maybe it would soothe my wounded ego that Heath had any interest in me.

TWO

Spells are fairly intense. In all the movies I'd ever seen, the witches just say a little chant, like, "No big deal, here are some words," Cue the smoke and poof! Whatever they wanted to have happen did.

Not an accurate account from what I was reading in these books. They involved body parts and vials of things, then days of simmering the concoction. But these weren't the simple spells. It was the big stuff, like seeing into the future and impersonating another person or witch.

My mom had enough vials of ingredients back at the house. I'd have to try one of these spells out on my next day off.

I'd stopped to grab a cup of coffee, no milk, two sugars, and I could feel it breathing life into my limbs as I took a sip.

Strolling into the basement precinct, I set down my dictionary of *tvary*. I had taken to carrying it just about everywhere since I'd found it, waiting to use it for more things than dead bodies. At least I hoped the *tvary* wasn't just for dead bodies.

"What do we have going on today?" I asked, sitting down in my chair and swiveling so I could see Tork.

"Not a whole lot. There was a break-in down in the south end of the city, but they found it was just a woman who'd locked herself out."

"Neighbors couldn't tell it was her?" I asked before taking a long swig.

Tork shrugged. "They didn't get a good look at her until Gonzalez got there."

"It's crazy how much slower we've been lately. I feel like we were hopping the first six weeks I was here."

Tork gave me a half-smile. "To be honest, it's kind of refreshing. No one is breathing down our necks right now, which is a change."

"What about the Mayor? You love talking to him." I teased him about his relationship with Heath daily. It always made whatever I was dealing with at the time seem a little lighter.

There was something to be said for his loyalty, because Tork would do anything to help the leader of his pack. I'd figured out the limit though, when I'd gotten a warrant to search Heath's mansion in connection with the Lee Vance murders.

The elevator dinged and heavy footsteps walked toward the desks.

"You're both here early," Heath said.

"Speak of the devil," I said under my breath. Heath shot me a glare and then a look of confusion, probably wondering what we'd been talking about.

"What brings you to the dungeon?" I asked, grinning up at him.

His scowl deepened and he shook his head. "I just thought I'd tell you the plans to create the jail have been approved by the city. Well, to be technical, by the paranormal city council."

I perked up. It had to be tiring to be him, having to deal with the human councils as well as appeasing the paranormals.

"Where are they building it?" Tork asked. I was dying to know as well. Hopefully it would be a maximum security one where our criminals wouldn't be able to escape while being transported to another facility.

"In order to keep peace and to stay within the bounds of the city, the vampire covens have agreed to donate a portion of their land to build the prison."

"Look at you, Master Negotiator," I said, tipping my coffee cup back again. I'd said it more out of surprise than anything, but the look of satisfaction on Heath's face flipped my insides and sent them running around like a kid on a sugar high.

"I'm surprised I even got a compliment out of you," he said, leaning against my desk. "But the better news is we're also going to expand the cells you have here, adding ten more in the process."

"We are definitely bursting at the seams right now with all the crime going on." Heath rolled his eyes at my typical sarcasm.

Tork nodded. "We need it. Then we don't have to do mind control with the regulars upstairs."

"We can use mind control?" I asked, wondering if this was yet another aspect of paranormal police work I needed to be clued in on.

The two guys looked at me like I had ten heads.

Instead of answering, Heath turned to Tork. "Are you ready for the Games?"

"Oh yeah. I'm taking down Gronski this year." Tork smiled wider than I'd seen in weeks. Stacia, his girlfriend and the city coroner, had been buried in work from the humans and I'd barely even seen them together, which was saying something. In a weird way, I missed the squirmy, romantic side of Tork.

"What Games?" I pictured the two of them in pinstripes playing old man softball or something like that. Scrub it from my brain. Heath would probably fill out the pants and I didn't need that thought distracting me.

"The Shifter Games," Heath said, turning to me. "It's the chance for the shifters to move up and down in rank within the pack, as well as teach the young ones. It's the highlight of the year." He grinned, the look more mischievous than anything I'd seen from him before. "You should come. It'll be a chance for you to learn some new moves. Maybe one day you'll be able to take on a shifter."

I frowned, wishing I could punch him right now. He'd made fun of my defensive skills since I'd arrived, but I'd already survived two crazy people with what I'd learned at the police academy.

"I'll come. It'll be fun watching you get your ass handed to you."

The comment would have carried more weight if I'd been able to stop smiling, but I couldn't resist as Heath gave me his sultry look of confidence.

He swaggered up to me and whispered, his hot breath on my ear making me shiver. "I never lose when I want something."

He turned and walked toward the elevator, and it was like I'd been frozen in time, just standing there trying to get my heart to beat a little slower.

Tork's laugh brought me around and I shook my head, not wanting to hear what he said about me having the hots for the Mayor. This was all a game we were playing and I had to make sure the feelings never went too deep.

THREE

The Shifter Games.

I'd never seen anything quite like it, and I'd been to at least one game of every sports team in Boston over the course of my life. Boston fans had some loyalty to their teams, but the extent of this was mind-blowing.

They set the arena up in the middle of the shifter lands, which extended back behind the Mayor's house for miles. Newton and Gonzalez were set to come after checking on a domestic disturbance call, while Tork and I drove together.

"This is where you all compete?" Of course, if Heath was in charge of something, he never did it halfway. We'd driven through a manicured section of trees that opened up to the large arena, the design of the columns a strange twist on the ones used in Rome back in the day.

"Yep, it was built about ten years ago. The one we had before was falling apart."

Signs for the participants and fans split off into different directions, and I pointed back to the one that said *Fans*, thinking he'd missed it.

"I know it's hard to believe, Beckett, but I'm competing as well."

I raised an eyebrow and shook my head. "You? What are you going to do? Wear your glasses and order people around?"

Despite the irritation I could see in his eyes, he shook his head and chuckled. "All I'd have to do is get a cup of coffee and constantly ask, 'Isn't there a database we can search for this?'" He made his voice go higher, and while I didn't agree with the volume of the imitation, his words were Claire Beckett to a tee.

At least I'd been able to get my *tvary* dictionary to make investigating easier. No, it wasn't searchable with lightning speed, but I could go for the "for sure" definition compared to winging it and hoping I was right.

He pulled into a parking spot a few rows down. To be honest, I'd never seen so many vehicles in one place. Okay, maybe Logan International Airport, but I didn't go there often when I lived in Boston.

People milled about in various states of dress and transformation. Fur or feathers sprouted on some, while others had completely transformed.

"How is it there are so many shifters?" I was in awe at the sheer number of the shifter pack here. "And are you all in different packs, since not all animals and birds are of the same species?"

Tork blinked slowly, his tell for the fact I was tiring him out with all the questions. "All the shifters in Crescent City are one pack. There are distinct divisions among us, such as Captain Woods is in the parliament of owls. They have a leader who reports to the shifter council."

That made sense. I tried to think of any more questions, but none came to mind.

Tork pulled a duffle bag out of the trunk and started toward the arena. I took a few quick steps to catch up, my gaze taking in the vibrant colors and the amount of fan paraphernalia being carried inside.

"Is Stacia coming today?" I asked, watching a small wolf bounce alongside its mother.

"No," Tork said, his lips pursing and his eyes narrowing in on something in front of us. "She had to work."

"For real? How many bodies have piled up in the human world over the past few days?" The human world wasn't something I thought about often anymore. Everything I needed was usually now part of the paranormal community, except the occasional phone call from my half-sister, Nina. And the odd appearance of Mrs. Samuels the other night.

"I'm not sure, but hopefully she can find a pattern to help the detectives upstairs." We walked forward several more steps before he said, "There was a body with some burns in the midsection, but they found the man in the boiler room of one of the factories. At least there wasn't a hole in the head, right?"

I laughed, surprised by Tork's little inside joke. We'd looked at plenty of burned holes on my first case here in the city and I was okay if those never cropped up again.

We made it inside the arena where several areas were roped off, signs directing spectators to their various sections. Large sides of cooked and uncooked meats hung from wires, along with carts of drinks and souvenirs. The stadium was set up as big as a football field, and if I didn't know better, I'd think we were at a professional game of sorts.

"How many shifters ARE there in Crescent City?" I asked, trying not to let my mouth hang open too long.

"Four or five hundred thousand. Something like seventy-five percent of them live here in the shifter lands, but the rest live among the humans."

I'd looked up the population of the city the first week I got here and it had said the city held roughly a million people. I guess it didn't account for all the species the humans couldn't see.

His comment about the shifters living with the humans made me think of the vampire girl I'd questioned on our last case. She lived among the humans and worked stocking shelves, which was a risk, but did so to get a break from her kind.

I glanced around the stadium, watching several animals running back and forth, stretching out as if this were an Olympics. With all the equipment set up, it might as well have been.

Dumbbells and shot puts, along with a sizable wall holding dozens of weapons, were all lined up against the wall across from me. A few of them looked similar to those in my mother's cottage, and I hoped I'd be able to see them in action, because I had no idea how to wield them.

Shifters filled in the stadium seating. When I turned to say something to Tork, I saw him already across the field.

"Where are you going?" I asked, jogging to catch up to him. Once I stopped, I tried to take in shallow breaths, not wanting him to see I was practically wheezing from the quick sprint.

"Don't worry, Beckett. The air is thinner here." He grinned and gave me a quick slap on the back. He then pointed to the doorway leading underneath the arena and said, "Best not follow me in here. The locker rooms are for competitors only. No need to see shifters without their clothes on."

Too many mental pictures ran through me and I stepped back, cringing. The last thing I needed to think about was Heath being among them, sans clothing.

"Where should I go, then?" I asked, feeling out of place with all the unknowns. It was cool to be here, but I also was out of my element, something I thought I'd be used to by now with all the changes in my life over the past few months.

"Wherever you want. It might be good to stay down here

near the field. Then you can get a look at the techniques we use to fight each other."

I nodded, spinning to look around the rest of the field. It looked as though they had things to throw, space to run, and a large box at the other end of the field, shrouded in a black cloth.

"Grab some food, Beckett," Heath said from behind me.

When I turned to face him, he was trying to look serious. "If I eat the raw meat, will I turn into a shifter?" I said it with a straight face, but the disgusted expression Heath shot in my direction caused me to laugh.

"Please, you wish you were a shifter," he said, stretching his arms across his chest.

"Who says I'm not?" I said, shrugging. "I healed from an ankle injury with lightning speed."

"You could be many things. Any luck finding your family tree?" He didn't have to say anything about the cottage for me to understand what he meant.

"Not quite. Plenty of spell books. The *tvary* dictionary has been awesome so far, but I haven't found a neat little pedigree of the Beckett-Sanchez clan. I was able to give the guys upstairs a clue about one of their cases, though."

It had been a lot harder working with the humans again. Not that I really worked with them. They all thought I was stationed in the records room, but a small tip about the victim's eyes had helped them close the case.

When I was with Tork or Newton, even Heath, I could speak freely and didn't have to come up with some lame reason I thought it was a robbery or a family member who'd committed the crime.

"Too bad we don't know your father's name," Heath said, tugging on some cleats that had more spikes than the one I was used to seeing.

"Do you not shift to compete?" I asked, pointing down at

the cleats. Maybe I hadn't gotten past the movie version of what shifters were supposed to be, but I was pretty sure they shed every article of clothing.

"I shift everything but my feet. They need the support from the cleats."

"You and Tork sound like you're getting ready for an old folk's home," I said, trying not to smile.

Instead of retorting, he walked up to me, the proximity causing my stomach to turn flips while my heart went haywire. He'd done this before, had gotten close and I'd thought he would kiss me but instead said something to rile me up.

"Do I look like I'm ready for an inhaler?" he whispered, making me shudder as the hot air of it tickled my ears.

And just like that, Claire Beckett was tongue-tied. Great.

He stepped back toward his bag, pulling out a large water bottle and taking a long swig. "Back to our conversation, do you know anything about your father?"

My mom had only mentioned my father once, back when I was eight or nine. She'd been talking to someone on the phone and I'd overheard her say, "Yes, Henry is Claire's father."

"All I've got is Henry." Once the words were out of my mouth, I sucked in a deep breath, realizing Henry was an even more popular name than Adelaide.

Heath raised an eyebrow and stood. Instead of his usual sarcastic words to match mine, he said, "Keep looking. I'm sure your mom left something somewhere. My father said she was very meticulous, keeping notes of everything."

I nodded, knowing it was true. She had at least forty volumes of journals and I knew it couldn't be all of them, because there were some still stashed in the storage shed back in Boston. I'd have to go there at some point and clear it out. My home was here now, and I didn't plan on heading back to Boston too often.

Heath nodded his head and jogged away, my eyes drifting down to his ass as he joined several other shifters. Damn, he was hot.

Half of them were already in their animal forms, but Heath was still a head taller than most of them, even when not fully shifted.

I glanced around the arena and found a spot where I could get a good watch of the events. My phone rang, and I glanced down, surprised to see Nina's name on the screen. The last time I'd spoken to her was a few weeks ago after Tori's death.

"Hey Nina," I said, trying to keep a casual tone.

"Where are you? I've been calling the past few days, and the number keeps going straight to voicemail."

Nice to talk to you too, sis.

"Um, yeah, I'm in a new area," I said, pacing back and forth. How did I tell my sister they had transferred me to Crescent City where I'd found several threads to our mother's past life? "Sometimes the cell service is spotty."

"What part of Boston doesn't have good cell service anymore?"

I hesitated, trying to come up with something.

But, in true Nina fashion, she didn't wait long to continue. "I'm actually coming back to town for a bit and wanted to meet up. I fly in tomorrow and should be there for several days. Do you have time to grab lunch or dinner together?"

I was in shock. My sister was asking me to have dinner with her. I'd always been a pain in the ass in her mind, the non-perfect sister who usually ruined her plans.

"Um, sure, yeah," I said, trying to remember my schedule for the next week. Christmas had been two days earlier, and we were working with a skeleton shift.

"I have to work tomorrow, but I can meet you on Tuesday. Does that work?"

"Definitely. Okay, I've got to get packing, but I'll see you then. Maybe we can walk the Freedom Trail or something."

I chuckled. "Nina, it's winter. No one walks the trail right now. We'd be icicles by the end."

Nina laughed, something I had only heard directed at me a handful of times in my life. What had happened to her and why was she being nice to me?

"I forget since it's still so nice out here. Okay, we'll find a way to catch up. See you then."

The line went dead, and I stared at my phone for several seconds, wondering if I'd just been duped or if she was really my half-sister.

A whistle blew, and the group of shifters had congregated in the middle of the field. A fox shifter held a microphone.

"We welcome you to the two-hundredth meeting of the Crescent City Shifter Games. We'll begin with the youth events and move into the adult ones. Remember, there is plenty of meat and food along the upper decks and we hope you enjoy this year's challenges."

Challenges? That made it sound a lot more intense than just a little competition.

Did it mean they tried to kill each other to move up in the shifter rankings?

FOUR

Death wasn't far off for some contestants. I'd never seen a place with so much action and violence in my life. The medical squad was constantly moving around, carting injured runners and fighters off the field so the competition could continue.

But as much as I enjoyed the events, it was the smaller shifters who drew me. The way they could pick up and toss creatures twice their size was fascinating. It would feel awesome to beat the shit out of a shifter if the opportunity ever arose, but alternative tactics would be my only hope for victory in that situation.

I stood next to the older kids, the ones who were probably teenagers, and learned how to fight for a few hours, practicing moves several times to imitate what they were doing.

"Why are you all in your human form learning to fight?" I asked the girl standing next to me.

She looked a bit scared, her nose turning into a bright yellow beak. I could understand the hesitation, since I was unfamiliar. Stranger danger must go across cultures.

Her nose changed back, and she said, "We learn to fight in

both forms. Then we're prepared for a fight whether we shift or not."

"That's a great reason. You shift into a bird?" I asked, wondering how she would fight.

She nodded. "I'm a Starling. The tactics are a lot different from wolves and the bigger animals, but I've won a few fights over the past year." She was practically beaming with pride as she said, "I'm Talia."

"I'm Claire. Nice to meet you."

The instructor of the youth started speaking again, demonstrating several other moves that were ten times better than what I'd learned in the Police Academy. Twisting out of a tight grip or even using my surroundings to escape. Vance's face kept flashing in my mind and I knew this time, if he were to attack me, I'd be better prepared to get away from him.

When the lessons were over for the youth, I sat in a lower box with some of them, watching as the adult shifters began their competitions.

"He's my favorite," Talia said, pointing toward the group. The mass of bodies and creatures was hard to make out which 'he' she was talking about.

"Who?" I asked, leaning closer so I might have a better look at where she was pointing.

"The wolf shifter, Mayor Heath." It took a moment for my eyes to register the brown-red coat of the wolf as being Heath, but his size and the cleats on his feet gave him away.

I smiled and turned to Talia. "Why is he your favorite?"

Talia's cheeks turned a bright pink, making her appear younger than I'd thought earlier. "Because he's the best leader we could have asked for. He's working hard to unite the paranormal world. Maybe we can go to the regular schools with the humans someday." She stopped a moment and then leaned closer, whispering, "And he's good-looking."

After a quick laugh about the last phrase, I sobered. I hadn't thought about the impact of schooling on the younger shifters. "Do you not have good schools in the shifter lands?"

"Oh no, they're good, I'm just fascinated with all things human." She laughed and I grinned, knowing how it is to be a teenager and dream of all the things that could be different about life. Little did I know how much different my life would become than the one I'd pictured years ago.

The group of shifters stepped up to the starting line and waited for the gunshot, sending them racing around the track. Inwardly, I cheered for Heath as he strode out in front of the rest of the group, a mixture of several animals. Around the last turn, it looked like the leopard was going to catch him, but Heath turned his legs even faster, breaking across the finish line in time to take first.

"So, did he win?" I asked Talia, curious about the process for the rest of the Games. If there was only one event, this was a lot of work for so little competition.

Talia nodded. "Just that heat. He'll have to compete in several others to earn the one hundred points to be crowned the winner of the Shifter Games."

"How many times has he won?" I asked, watching him cool down as he waved to the crowd.

"Eight in a row. It's the reason everyone always listens to him, even when there's a major argument. They know he's the one to beat every year."

Eight years going through all this. It looked like there were several who were out to take his spot at the top. Not that I didn't like him leading the shifters, with the energy he seemed to have for all the causes in this city, maybe more time away from leadership roles would be good for him. As Mayor of the city, both humans and paranormals, leader in the bodyguard firm, as well as my full-time protector, I wondered when he got sleep.

In the next heat, I recognized Levi Tomlinson, a shifter we'd interviewed when trying to figure out who was killing the heads of the vampire covens.

He was fairly fast, but didn't have the smooth gait Heath had shown, coming in second place.

Several hours later, the numbers were tied between Heath and the Leopard. How was this going to end?

Only one event left, and we'd know who won.

A scream came from behind me. By the time I turned, all I saw was a small red bird with holes in its chest and stomach.

"Fletcher," Talia said, jumping off the bench and running back to pick him up.

I held her back, knowing if this had been a body, we'd need to investigate it before contaminating evidence.

"Did anyone see anything?" I asked the crowd of youth.

"His shirt started smoking and then he changed into his bird form." A girl trembled as she tried to speak.

"What do you mean his body started smoking? Like it was on fire?" I asked, trying to figure out how it would work while completely surrounded with other shifters.

The girl nodded and I turned, detective mode initiating.

I sprinted toward Tork and Heath, grateful they were in the same area. "I think we've got a murder."

"What?" the two of them asked at the same time.

"A young boy shifted into his bird form and there are holes burned through his chest and abdomen."

A wildness caught in Heath's eyes and he turned, lifting a microphone from the stand in the middle of the field.

"Security, please lock down the facility." The crowd murmured, all eyes riveted on us in the middle. "We'll post-pone the last race."

He dropped the mic, looking like he was ready to pummel someone for causing this to happen now.

"How did this happen?" he asked, glaring at me.

I shrugged, frowning at his silent accusation I was behind it. "I was with the younger shifters and we heard a scream. When I turned around, I found the bird on the ground."

We'd narrowed the distance between where the guys were standing and where the body had been found.

As I squatted down and stared at the small bird, I wondered what would have hit him that would burn through him as well as cause him to shift from human to bird. And with all of us sitting around the area.

"None of the shifters can do something like this," Heath said, glancing between Tork and myself. "We can at least let them all go."

I glanced up at the crowd, many of the people watching us discuss the incident. This wasn't my call, but from the sheer number of people in the stadium, we'd be here for days researching and interviewing.

Tork rubbed his face with his palms, the hair on the back of his hands thickening. He turned and confronted me with words I never thought I'd hear him say. "He's right. None of the shifters have the power to burn."

For several seconds, the air left my lungs as I went through the implications. "Y-you don't think I did that, do you?" There had been no power surge through my body, which was how I could tell I was about to produce electricity. At least that's what happened the last two times I'd used it.

Tork's eyes went wide, and he said, "No, of course not. I'm just saying, do you think we should let the crowd go home?"

"Isn't the point to figure out who did this? And don't you agree they were most likely in the arena when it happened?" My insides were at war with hoping to go home and soak in a bubble bath to ease the muscles after all I'd learned today, and knowing justice depended on our diligence.

Heath glanced at Tork, his expression giving away nothing. He wanted to protect his people as much as anyone else, but was there another reason he wanted everyone to leave?

"I'll get started on the first section over here," Tork said, motioning toward the stands above us.

I grabbed onto his upper arm and gave him a quick smile. "For fear of sounding like a broken record, is there some technology we can consult first?" There had been an intense security system I'd seen the fans go through, and it might give us a few more clues than we'd had before.

Newton and Gonzalez appeared out of nowhere. If we were going to interview thirty thousand shifters, we could use every person we had available.

"Nice of you two to show up when it's become a crime scene," Tork remarked.

"Well, Boss," Newton said, glancing down at the bird on the ground, "This isn't the first victim. We found five other birds in a similar condition on our way back from the domestic disturbance."

"Where?" Tork and I asked at the same time.

"Two were at the roundabout by the entrance to the city. The other three were just a few blocks away. We stopped because of the group of people surrounding them."

Tork glanced between the two of them and asked, "What did you do with the bodies?"

Gonzalez nodded and said, "We took them to Stacia. She said she was almost done with the last human autopsy and would get on it right away."

"Let them go, Mayor," Tork said, squatting down to look at the bird.

It didn't take long for the people to vacate the premises, and the stadium was eerie without all the people.

"Where do we start, Boss?" Newton asked.

Tork stared at me for several seconds, causing me to squirm somewhat until he cracked a grin. "We're going to follow Beckett's suggestion. Let's look for cold cases, cases with anything similar in our database. Beckett and Newton, head back to the precinct to start on that. Gonzalez and I will go through the security footage in the hopes we'll find something."

I cringed, grateful I hadn't been assigned to watch video for hours. It would be like finding a needle in a shifter pack.

FIVE

I don't know why I kept thinking our computer systems would be up to par with what we needed to search for in every case. Using any form of burn in the police database turned up absolutely nothing helpful. I'd worn out the online thesaurus with terms we could use to describe the burns and the dead birds, but nothing came up.

Tork and Gonzalez hadn't had any luck finding suspects either, and I was hoping some evidence would appear so we wouldn't have to shelve this case already.

And now it was time to meet up with my sister. In the city where my attacker, Lee Vance, was hiding out.

I had the bottom of my blouse twisted around my finger, trying to breathe as Heath drove us into the city.

"Are you going to be okay?" Heath asked from the driver's seat. He kept threatening I'd be getting a different protector, but he was still on the job, and to be honest, it was kind of a relief. We had a predictable relationship; I would badger him until he got frustrated, and he'd annoy me by calling me Miss Beckett from time to time.

"I'll be fine," I said, not taking my eyes off the road.

"You've been really quiet the past two hours. Which would normally be a good thing," Heath said, reaching over to turn down the sound on the radio a bit, "but this has been a little weird, even for you."

I rolled my eyes at him and turned to glance at the car next to us. The driver looked over and for a second, my heart stopped, sure I'd just seen Lee Vance grinning at me. I blinked and saw the man driving was old. It should have made me feel more comfortable, but I wondered if Lee had changed himself to look like that, only to make me fret for the entire trip.

"You didn't just see Lee Vance in the black car, did you?" I said, pointing to the vehicle. It sped up, making it impossible to see the driver's face.

"No, Beckett. But if he does come after you, at least you're not going into the city alone."

I nodded, doing the breathing exercises Dr. Stringer had given me a few weeks ago. They usually helped settle me down, but in this case, my nerves continued to fray.

"Have you seen the therapist again?" Heath mentioned, his voice low and growly.

Damn, why did he have to do that? Did he have telepathy? He usually guessed exactly what I was thinking. It wouldn't be ideal if so, since my attraction levels spiked whenever I was around him. At least the butterflies helped take the edge off the anxious knots in my stomach.

"Yes," I said. I picked at my fingernails, not wanting to see his reaction.

"And?"

"What are you? My father?" I said, irritation burning in my chest.

Heath slammed on the brake, avoiding an accident with a

car that had slowed down much more than it should have. The other lanes were clear.

"If that's what's going to keep you safe, then yes, I'll be an authority figure in your life." His eyes flashed a warning, and I sucked in a breath, waiting for what would come next. "Or, news flash, we could actually be friends. You know what that means, right, Beckett?"

His words sliced through my emotions, reminding me of all I'd lost in the past few months.

Friends with Heath. Was it even possible?

"Dr. Stringer thinks I have PTSD, but she needs a few more sessions to decide whether I need meds." I stared at him, watching every emotion play across his face. At least he wasn't gloating.

"See? That wasn't hard at all. I know I'm no Tori, but you can at least try to be open."

His casual mention of my deceased best friend's name created questions.

"How well did you know Tori?" I asked, curiosity bubbling to the surface.

"Really well. We grew up together and then we were in the same training class for the protector position."

"Wait, how old are you then?"

"Twenty-seven."

I clamped my teeth shut so my jaw didn't drop to my hands. He was only a year older than me? All he'd done for the city in such a short amount of time sent a feeling of shame through me. I'd done little more than become a cop. But at least I'd made it this far. The past eight years had demanded a hell of a lot from me, and I was proud of the fact I'd made it here, with the title of detective.

"What does a shifter have to do to become a bodyguard?"

Heath placed his left hand on top of the steering wheel and

leaned his right elbow on the console, bringing him inches closer to me and sending a whiff of his decadent cologne my way.

"Most *protectors* are chosen from their schools," he said, emphasizing the word protector. "There were ten of us in total, seven still in the line of work."

"So how did you become the head of the shifters, the head of the bodyguard group, and the mayor? Just trying to take on the world all at once?" I added my typical sarcastic flare, but I was mostly curious about how one guy could have time for it all.

Heath laughed, shaking his head as he stared out at the road in front of us. He swerved in front of an oncoming car and made it in time to get back over, past the car that stopped.

"I'm not the leader of all those things. Yes, I'm the mayor, and yes, my family has led the shifters for generations, but I'm not the head of the Shifter Guard."

"I thought—"

"You assumed. I have some say in certain things and I am a manager of a region of protectors, but I'm not the big guy when it comes to calling all the shots. I've recommended Levi Tomlinson as your protector because I think he needs the challenge and you could whip him into shape, personality-wise."

"Great." That was news to me. Having a babysitter who I was actually having to teach things to did not sound like my idea of a protector, though. The great thing about Heath was he gave me enough room so I didn't feel smothered, but he usually knew where I was or at least what I was up to.

"What time do you have to meet your sister?" Heath asked, glancing at the clock on the dash.

"Noon. She wanted to go to a place in the North End."

"Pasta. It's always an excellent choice."

I flicked him with the back of my hand, connecting with his

bicep. Damn, he was strong, and I had to tamp down the urge to touch his arm again. "There are more restaurants than just pasta. There are several places that serve Latino food."

"Where did she want you to meet?" With his lopsided grin, I couldn't help but smile.

"She picked pasta."

We both laughed for several seconds and then settled into a calm quiet. We were in the city and the tightness in my chest was like my lungs sucking in air from a pea-sized hole.

What if Lee knew I was coming back into the city? What if he was waiting to attack me all for some book he thought I had?

I mentally worked through the few skills I'd learned while at the Shifter Games, hoping I'd be able to survive any encounter with more confidence, since I couldn't control when I released electricity.

Heath maneuvered through the traffic like it was early morning, allowing us to arrive two minutes early. And we found a parking spot across the street from the restaurant, something I'd never done the few times I'd taken my car out of the parking garage while living in the city.

Heath sat in the car and I asked, "Aren't you coming?"

"I don't want to interrupt your reunion. But I'll be out here if you need anything. It might be a good idea to get her to come to your storage shed before we move it all back to Crescent City."

"What do you mean, move it all?" I paused, one foot out of his car with the other foot waiting. We'd talked about me heading to the storage shed while we were here but moving it all hadn't been a conclusion.

"You might as well have all your things close, don't you think? And if Vance is after something, you'll know he's trying to take it from you when it's closer than three hours away."

I frowned. "Thanks for that. Just what I wanted to have happen. Lee Vance coming after me again."

"I can call off the movers if you want me to," he said, pulling his phone out of his pocket.

"You got movers? Where the hell am I going to store all of it? There's no way my apartment can hold a hundred boxes or more." My apartment was spacious right now, but having all the boxes stacked to the roof of the shed inside it would make me look like one of those hoarders I'd seen on TV.

And my mom's cottage had little room to work with either. Not to mention I'd have to move it all in by myself, because... no people.

"I've got space in my shed out back. We can put it in there temporarily."

I blinked a few times, trying to get the conversation to compute. "You've got space? You don't have dozens of cars lined up in there?"

"Have you seen me drive more than two cars?" he asked with a smile.

I shook my head and stepped out of the car. "You made me late. Don't get too bored."

"I never do when I have to watch you, Claire," he said, giving me an odd smile.

What was that supposed to mean?

SIX

He's just my protector. He's just my protector.

I practically chanted it on my way into the restaurant. My brain wasn't listening as it kept repeating the way he'd said my first name. As much as I didn't want to, I would probably analyze it for days to come.

The guy was good. He knew all the right buttons to push, getting my emotions to go from sixty to zero or vice versa.

I opened the door of The Lil Pie, my senses blasted with the smell of onions and garlic. A quick glance around the dining room told me Nina hadn't arrived yet, which was irregular for her. The girl could have her picture put on Wikipedia for being chronically early to everything. Maybe a bit of it had rubbed off on me over the years.

"How many?" a woman asked, shuffling up to me from what looked to be the kitchen in the back of the restaurant.

"Two." I lifted two fingers to help emphasize it when she looked confused. She took the menus from the small box at the side of the podium and waved for me to follow her.

Once seated at the side of the restaurant, she recited the

specials and walked off, leaving me glancing every few seconds toward the door. There weren't a ton of patrons, but they'd just opened for the day.

The bell above the door dinged, and I glanced up to see my half-sister, her usual blonde hair a darker shade of brown now. What would have caused her to stop dying it? It was the signature Nina Sinclair, the blonde hair always in its place, her clothing always on brand and neat as a pin.

She turned and found me, walking my way in her clicking heels and pantsuit set.

"Hey Nina," I said, sliding out and giving her a quick hug. It was weird to do so, but I was sort of out of it being back in Boston after all that had happened here.

She slid into the other side of the booth. "Wow, it's been a long time. I can't believe how long your hair is now." I'd worn my hair straight today, and I'd played with it more than ever, as it kept tickling my neck. That's what happened when I wore it in a ponytail, day after day.

"Yeah, it's nice to have it longer." The last time she'd seen me I'd had an A-line bob, a momentary lapse in judgment that ended in several months of trying to grow it back out.

Her features were softer than they usually were when directed toward me. "How have you been?"

The sincerity in her voice threw me and I paused, pinching my arm under the table to make sure I was actually living this moment and not in a dream. For a minute, I could pretend we weren't searching for a mysterious method to kill shifters, as well as a psychotic shapeshifter on the loose.

"Well, um, it's been a crazy couple of months." If she only knew half of it.

Nina lifted the menu up to glance at it and said, "Oh, really? Why?"

Now was the time to just come clean. "I got transferred to a new precinct and I've been working to get to know the area."

She forced a smile and said, "Are you in Southie, or around here?"

I bit my bottom lip, wondering what her reaction would be. "It's a place called Crescent City. It's about three hours from here."

Nina's eyes flew open wide, her attention glued to my face. "Wait, you moved to another city? I never thought I'd see that happen." She sat back, staring at me. "HOW did it happen?"

Maybe it was because she was acting more like a sister I could confide in than the guardian I'd had to put up with for years, but I wanted to confess it all to her. She and Heath would be an excellent match with those same abilities. I frowned, not wanting to think about Nina with the Mayor.

"I might have broken into the morgue at the Twenty-Seventh to see what they'd found out about Tori."

Nina's jaw dropped. This was the most surprised I'd ever seen her about anything, and a bit of pride rose that I'd been able to keep my nosy sister in the dark about the whole thing until I'd gotten settled.

"You broke into a government building and you're still a cop?"

I was about to correct her and say I was now a detective, to drive home the point she'd been wrong about me for years, but the title would ring too many warning bells for her and I needed to keep that much for a while. Nina would be back to California in no time anyway, so why not just keep this little omission? I'd admitted to all the other stuff.

"Yeah, I guess Captain Southwick knew Mom, so he pulled some strings as a payback for some debt he owed her," I said, thinking about his confession. She might've been alive now if he'd listened to her claims about the latest case she'd been working on.

"Wow, that's incredible. So, do you like this new place? Crescent City, did you say?"

The server took our orders, the lasagna for me and the shrimp scampi for Nina, and took off with the menus, leaving us to our conversation. I wondered if my entrée would be as good as my neighbor's.

"I didn't think I would, but I actually really love it there. I've had some interesting cases and have settled into my apartment."

"I still can't wrap my brain around Claire Beckett living outside the city of Boston. It suits you." She gave me a genuine smile and tears might have appeared, burning the side of my eyes. I held them back and glanced down at my glass of water, focusing on taking the paper off the straw until I'd gotten them under control.

What a revelation. I hadn't realized I'd preen like this from a compliment Nina gave me.

After taking a sip of water, I said, "What brings you back to Boston? Did you shorten your Christmas vacation with Brad's family?"

Nina and Brad had dated ever since she'd arrived in California, and she'd called me several times from family functions over the past few years.

"Brad and I broke up, about two weeks ago," Nina said, swallowing hard. "It was for the best. Things hadn't been good with us in quite a while and things... well, let's just say he didn't understand all I was going through."

That piqued my interest. Brad seemed like the All-American match to Nina's perfect TV persona, although it was hard to picture now that her hair wasn't dyed blonde. But she looked more sophisticated with the brown locks, more like Mom.

"I'm sorry, Nina. It's always hard."

She glanced up at me and then back down at my hand covering hers.

"Yeah, you know how it is. But I'd rather know now than commit to life together and be miserable." She pulled out a compact from her purse, dabbing a little cover up over her nose and chin. She'd always worried about her appearance, but this seemed to be more excessive than in the past.

Was she nervous about something? About meeting with me?

Our food came and we ate in silence for a bit. It was official: Mrs. Samuels' lasagna beat this one out of the water. Still good, but it was lacking a spice or two.

"I'm glad you came out, Nina. This feels good, getting together and talking." I leaned back, using the edge of my fork to cut through the layers of pasta and cheese. "I definitely enjoy talking to you as a sister and not as a mom-figure."

Nina laughed and nodded. "It's nice to know I didn't completely screw things up. And I know you hated me there for a while, but I was doing the best I knew how. It was hard enough to deal with Mom's death and then suddenly become a single parent."

"Well, I wasn't always the easiest to deal with." I picked up my water and took a sip. A peace settled into my chest, the hope maybe I wouldn't be alone in this life forever. Sure, I had the new people I'd met in Crescent City, but there was still a lot those people didn't know about me. What if they were killed just by associating with me? Or what if they abandoned me once they realized who I really was, once I found out, that is?

"What are your plans for the next couple of weeks?" Nina asked, stabbing a piece of penne and taking a bite.

I raised an eyebrow, trying to figure out why she would still be here for that amount of time. She'd only been home as long as four or five days when she'd been back in the past.

"Work, mostly. When do you have to head back to California?" I stared at her, trying to decide what had happened to my sister. She was so goal-oriented that to even have things not planned out to a T seemed off. She hadn't been taken over by anyone, right?

Please don't let her be Lee Vance.

Nina blew out a breath. "That's the thing. I kind of lost my job."

I blinked several times, trying to decide what to make of this revelation. Nina failed at something?

"Wait, what?" My brain kept stuttering over it, like the facts wouldn't translate to my language.

She closed her eyes and almost shuddered before opening them to stare at me. For a second, I thought I saw a flicker of blue in them, but I blinked too quickly and her regular brown eyes stared back.

"A few weeks ago, I started having this strange dream about an old woman and what looked like a small metal stick. She was waving it in the air and trying to talk to me, but there was something against her throat that kept her from saying anything. Brad was a bit freaked out about it, but what could I do? This was all new to me."

I leaned forward, curious what the dream could mean. If it had just been once, it wouldn't have mattered as much, but several times and the same dream?

"Did you get a look at what she was holding?"

Nina shook her head. "Nothing clear. I only saw a couple of gems in the middle, and then three rings all tied together, like those old school locks?" She moved her hand as if she were unlocking a door, and I immediately thought of the key Sloan had given me to my mother's cottage weeks ago.

"Is it the size of a key?" I asked, trying not to pat my pocket, where the key was tucked right now.

"No, it looked bigger."

"Did you hear anything the woman said?" Had this been connected to our family and she was seeing the paranormal world as well?

A strange zip of hope shot through me. Was it awful of me to want someone else who'd known me forever to understand what was going on? That I could guide through this new journey and then we could figure out the rest together?

"Just a few whispers here and there. They said something about finding it in Boston and now is the time."

The words made me shiver and I leaned back, trying to control my emotions. Maybe I wouldn't have to wait too long for her to understand we were from a paranormal world.

"You can stay with me for a few weeks until you figure out what you're going to do." Five years ago, I would've laughed at the idea of willingly sharing a dwelling with Nina again. But it seemed like she'd changed a lot, and I wanted to help with what little I could.

I just hoped this newfound relationship would continue.

I paid the check, and we stood, grabbing coats and belongings. After sitting in the warmth for so long, I wasn't ready for the frigid weather just outside the building.

"You'd be okay with me staying at your apartment?" Nina asked, doubt mixed with hope in her tone.

I shrugged. "Of course. We're family. And I could use family around me for a while."

We stepped outside the restaurant and stood on the sidewalk, staring at each other for a few seconds. Was I going to regret inviting her over? Memories of Nina the Guardian clouded my vision, and I just hoped she didn't slip back into the power-hungry, frustrated woman she'd been back then.

"I really appreciate it, Claire. More than you know."

I reached out and touched her arm. "What happened with your job?"

"Strange things. Accidents kept happening around the set whenever I was around. But I arrived late to the set five days in a row."

My jaw dropped and I'm pretty sure my eyes were as wide as possible. "You? Late to work?"

Instead of irritated, like she would be on a normal day, she nodded and frowned. "I know, right? I've always been a model of punctuality. But it was like I lost hours of time, and I'm not even sure what happened. I figured I might as well come back home and see if the dreams and the blackouts subsided."

All the details she'd shared with me were adding more and more anxiety. This wasn't just a coincidence. There had to be things involved with the paranormal world causing this. But what?

"Okay, I'll meet you back at your apartment?" Nina asked, pulling the strap of her purse and resting it on top of her shoulder.

And here it was, the official declaration I hadn't come to Boston alone. I motioned to the sleek black Maserati sitting next to the curb across the street. "He's my ride home."

As if he could hear me, okay, he probably could, Heath rolled down the window. "Are you ready?" he asked, looking at me.

A jerk on my arm caused me to glance back at Nina, who pulled me to face the buildings so our backs were to Heath. "What is going on? You moved out of Boston and you're with a guy who looks like he could be a bodybuilding model? What happened to you?" I'd never seen this much confusion and excitement coming from Nina, ever.

"They transferred me, remember?" I had told her, didn't I?

Or had we talked during one of her blackout episodes? "And the Mayor is just here as a guide. He, um, had to come into Boston today anyway, so it worked out."

A guide? It was the worst excuse on the planet, and Nina wouldn't buy it.

"You mean you two aren't a thing?" When I shook my head, she grinned. "Damn, girl, I don't know how you always get the super-hot ones to hang out with you and then nothing ever happens."

I rolled my eyes, hoping that Heath had stopped listening. What happened to all his mayoral duties? Couldn't someone call him right now and spare me the embarrassment?

"We're... friends," I said, trying to channel the conversation we'd had earlier. "Anyway, do you have a car or do you want to ride with us?"

"I have a rental I'll drive over there. I don't want to be stuck driving Sonja, unless you got a new car by now?" Her mild disgust at my car brought back the irritation I was used to with her. Oh yeah, there was no way a shapeshifter had taken her over. This was 100% Nina Sinclair.

"She's still running like she did when Mom died."

"Probably a good thing you didn't drive out here by yourself then. The highways would be rough to sit on for too long."

I shook my head, knowing she implied I would've been sitting there for a while if the engine overheated, despite the below freezing temperatures.

"We have to make a stop at storage and then we'll be ready to go. Do you have anything else you need to do in the city before we leave?" Part of me hoped we wouldn't have to trudge through the storage shed together, at least not today. I was already exhausted from all the pent-up anxiety from our meeting and the long drive ahead, that I didn't need to be sitting in a small dark square looking at trinkets for hours and then driving home.

"Beckett," Heath called out. "They're done. We can head back home now."

I jumped, wondering if he'd gotten a call about the movers or if he'd overheard us talking. Well, that was a relief. One less thing in my already packed schedule. It was hard enough having a day off and trying to get all the big stuff done.

But I was out of food so I'd still have to get groceries tonight. My favorite thing. I groaned just thinking about those aisles filled with too many options.

"I guess Heath got it resolved," I said, turning to Nina. "Where are you parked?"

"Up around the corner. I'm in a tan compact car. Just wait a moment and I'll meet you back here."

"Do you want me to ride with you?" I asked, wondering if she'd be okay following Heath. He drove, well, like he wasn't part of the crowd and sometimes it was hard to keep up.

"Are you kidding? You ride with him. You need to get over Stetson Burton and he'd be the perfect start."

I closed my eyes and pinched the bridge of my nose. "Just let it go, all right?"

"You look just like Mom right there, you know? Although she usually pinched right there when she was annoyed with you."

Touché.

"Okay, well, try to keep up, then." I watched her turn and walk away and then walked back to the car.

"I take it your lunch went well?" Heath asked, a smile playing at his lips.

I took a deep breath, trying to figure out how I felt about it. Well wasn't the word to describe it.

"It was different. She's actually going to follow us home. So don't lose her."

"I gathered that much, but why is she coming to Crescent City?" Heath asked, turning the key in the ignition.

"She lost her job and broke up with her boyfriend. She's had some strange dreams and several blackouts, where she can't account for the hours lost. I think those added to the change of scenery." I bit my bottom lip, feeling the tingling I'd had ever since I'd gotten to Crescent City, like something was about to happen. "I'm not sure what or who it's from, but I know it's all connected."

Heath nodded. "After all I've learned, anything happening in your family is for a reason."

"What reason?"

"Whatever your mom did to the Shadowmoon Coven is coming back to get the two of you."

SEVEN

I couldn't get his words out of my head for the entire drive. Sure, we talked here and there, trying to decipher Nina's dream, but nothing stuck out to us. My brain switched gears back to my mother and why she'd taken the Codex from her coven.

"This is where you live now?" Nina asked, her voice filled with wonder as we stepped into the apartment. "You've definitely moved up from the garbage pile you lived in with Tori."

I flicked the light switch on to the hallway, guiding her to the extra bedroom. At least there was that. We might kill each other if we had to share a bedroom for too long and with my closet and one wall covered in everything I knew about my mother's and Tori's killer or killers, I didn't need her asking questions.

"Well, it's one perk of being a cop in this city, I guess." I motioned to the furniture. It was nicer than anything I'd ever had.

It being a perk wasn't entirely true. I was pretty sure Heath had a hand in getting me into this apartment, probably as a way to watch over me.

There was less crime around this building, anyway. I still wasn't sure where Tork, Newton, or Gonzalez lived. But Macee Butterfield, one of the regular human cops, lived several flights above me. Maybe it was the newbie section?

"This will be your room. I'll ask the lady down the hall if she has an air mattress or something."

Nina waved her hand in the air. "I'll just sleep on the couch tonight. Tomorrow I'll head to the store and grab a few things."

"Are you sure?" I asked, not sure I believed her.

"Claire, you don't have to worry about me. I'll stay out of your way as much as possible. I'm just grateful I have a place to stay until I figure out my life." I was used to high-maintenance Nina, not grateful, agreeable Nina.

I tried to hold back my curiosity, but it finally won out. "Did you feel anything in Boston? Anything connected to your dreams?"

Nina's expression fell, and she shook her head. "I wish I could say yes, or figure this all out and get back to life as usual, but there was nothing."

She turned and walked out to the front room, grabbing another piece of luggage. I wasn't sure how she'd gotten four suitcases on the plane and then into the compact car, but it seemed she'd packed up most of her worldly possessions to fly here.

"I'm sure you'll figure it out. And I have a few extra clearances here in Crescent City, so let me know if there's a lead you need me to track down or something." It was a stretch, but Tork had been lenient with finding out things about my mother. I hoped it extended to Nina as well.

"That would be great, since all the contacts I've built up

over the years are on the other side of the country." Nina's voice conveyed just how much she missed being in California, as it was totally her style. Sun, sand, beach, and the news usually revolved around celebrities.

"I need to run and get some groceries. Do you want to come?" I kind of hoped she'd say no, that she'd want to stay in and relax, but my luck didn't reach that far.

"Sure," she said, slipping her shoes back on. "It will help me get a grasp of the area."

We passed the mirror hanging on the far wall, and I couldn't help but smile at the differences between us. Nina, so prim and proper, me in my favorite leather jacket and jeans with small holes wearing out in the knees. But that was just us. We were Olivia's daughters, oil and water.

As I thought about our mother, I wondered how much Nina knew about my mother's past. Was she just as in the dark as I'd been?

"What are you thinking about?" Nina asked, breaking my train of thought.

"Nothing. Why?"

"You get a deep line in your forehead when you're trying to save the world." She waited a moment and said, "You should think about your chauffeur."

"I told you, Nina, he's off limits. He's the mayor of the town and I'm a cop. Besides, he's worth a gazillion dollars. I'm just grateful I got a pay raise when I got here. And the cost of living is cheaper, which helps." Try free for the foreseeable future.

"Women get guys with a higher social rank than themselves all the time. I think you'd be just fine, if you let it happen." She wiggled her eyebrows and gave me a half-smile.

The idea started to play out in my head, but my mind stopped it before the beginning credits rolled.

"Nina, can we stop talking about Heath? Let's just focus on

catching up and figuring out what's going on with your dreams, okay?"

My voice had an edge to it and Nina must have noticed because she nodded and leaned back in her seat, staring out at the road in front of us.

Once we made it to the parking lot, she said, "I'm surprised Sonja is still running. And this seat isn't as bad as I remember it."

I gave her a half-smile. "It's been like four years since you've been in my car. Maybe yours was bad."

We made it through the store in about thirty minutes, filling up the cart with many things until Nina finally went and got a second cart for her stuff.

We loaded it into the car and then carried it upstairs to my apartment. Nina said, "This makes me miss Mom even more. I remember doing this so many times. Hauling the groceries up to the apartment and then having to unload them all and put them away."

I nodded, remembering those simpler days. "Did Mom ever talk about living outside of Boston?" It was the safest question I could ask without stirring up confusion and curiosity.

Nina frowned. "No, I don't remember it. She just always said she lived by the water."

I pictured the house I'd made frequent trips to over the past few weeks, trying to see mentally if I'd noticed any kind of water around it. I'd need to find a map of the paranormal part of the city to narrow down the areas.

"Why do you ask?" Nina pulled out the bag of apples and set it on the counter next to the fridge.

"Oh, just some lady thought she knew who I was the other day. She called me Belinda Sanchez." I glanced down for a second, not wanting to tip off my half-sister Belinda was our mother's actual identity.

"Belinda Sanchez sounds familiar, but then again, I've worked with several Hispanics over the past few years at the network."

A flame of hope went out. No leads there. I needed to get back to the cottage and keep researching. It was bound to come up at some point, right?

As I prepared for bed, I thought about Nina, wondering what powers she had hidden deep. Maybe the dreams were part of her bruja abilities peeking through. Because we at least had our mother's genes in common. But what had her father been? A shifter? Warlock? A gargoyle like Newton?

I didn't have all the answers yet, but something told me I would find out in the coming days.

EIGHT

Rubbing my hands together after coming in from the cold, I waited for the coffeemaker to spit out the dark contents. I knew it was going to be bad, but I'd put myself on a weekly budget and daily coffee had been reduced to twice a week. Sonja wasn't going to last forever and since I didn't have to pay rent, with a little saving, I might be able to afford a better car soon.

I'd have to buy a coffee maker and start making my own at home the way I liked it, rather than whatever Tork did to the brew.

"How was your trip to the big city?" Tork asked, passing me to grab a paper from the printer on the shelf below.

"It made for a long day, but we got everything done. At least I think we did." It had been a relief to not have to move anything or go through the boxes, but I also hadn't been able to relax completely since Nina was staying with me. I'd covered up all the yarn spider webs on the one wall in my bedroom so she didn't think I was some serial killer stalking people.

Tork nodded. "Heath said your stuff nearly filled the last section of his shed."

Great. Just one more thing to add to my list of things to do. Find out who I am and who my mom was. Research what she did to the bruja coven. Find the person who killed her and Tori. And dejunk my stuff in Heath's shed. It was down there on the totem pole of tasks, but it needed to happen soon so I wasn't more in debt to Heath than I already was.

"Any action yesterday?" I hoped we had some new lead for the death of the bird boy. I needed something to do, something to investigate.

"Newton ran a list of cold cases and pulled the files. Maybe sort through there. We might find something connected to the murder."

"I was hoping you'd have found some solid leads given all the TV time you and Gonzalez have had," I said, giving him a nudge with my elbow. I didn't realize how much I'd missed investigating a murder after just a couple of quiet weeks. I shouldn't have been hoping for crime to happen just for my own amusement, but it was like I was going through with-drawals from the fast-paced few weeks when I first got here. Who knew, maybe I'd be wishing to go back to the slower pace soon.

I carried my coffee over to my desk. Tork had already stacked the files on the corner of it and I pulled the top one, reading it in between sips of the bitter liquid.

"Wait, did Stacia come up with a cause of death? And were all the injuries in the same area?"

Tork shook his head. "No cause of death. The injuries all looked the same, but the insides were different. Some were missing the heart and liver, while a few others had both lungs gone. Stacia is just as baffled as we are."

Woman killed in the woods near her home. I glanced at the pictures, seeing the wound in the upper chest and her side. A longer check around the body revealed no *tvary*.

The great thing about having found the dictionary in my mother's cottage was the fact it had one little section on how the *tvary* worked in the first few pages.

Different power levels cast the different colored symbols on the ground. Lee Vance had cast green because his powers were significantly higher than Lyra's, the vampire who killed all the heads of the three vampire covens. Hers had been yellow.

And after using some colored pencils to understand what the book was saying, I realized the power system went according to the colors of the rainbow, but in reverse, meaning purple was most powerful. The easiest way for me to remember was through the moniker Roy G. Biv. Red, orange, yellow, green, blue, indigo, violet.

When there was no evidence of *tvary*, it usually meant the killing was caused by a human, which is what I'd guessed happened to this woman.

"I found no *tvary* around this body. There was no mention of her paranormal abilities, so why do we have it?"

Tork walked over, chewing on what looked like a doggy treat, his lips smacking loudly behind me.

"She was a partial shifter. I think the system just tried to reach as far as possible. And a lot of these are cases we haven't been able to get to until now because of all that went into starting this division."

It was true. Captain Woods, Tork, and Heath had worked for over a year to build this division to what it was by the time I came aboard. I had worked all of one case, the one where we caught Vance, before they hired Newton, then Gonzalez shortly after. We were an odd bunch to look at, but we were coming together and no one could say we weren't effective.

"Have you gone through these files yet?" I asked, placing the woman's file to the side and grabbing the next from the top.

Tork shook his head, swallowing his snack and relieving my

ears from the crunching sound. "No, but I figured you'd have plenty to say or ask about along the way, so you're helping me out with this." He gave me a smile, more mischief than anything, and turned back to his desk.

"I wish Stacia could get you to understand empathy. Or at least when you're screwing over your partner."

"This is just part of the menial tasks I don't have time for."

An alarm rang on his phone and he picked it up, pointing to it with his other hand. "Meeting with the Captain about the case. Let me know what you find."

I let out a long breath and dove in, knowing the possibility of answers was within this stack. I just hoped it would lead to a conviction rather than a dead end.

NINE

A few hours into my search, I stood up and stretched, needing a break from the sheets of information on the background of each victim, as well as the coroner's reports and any testimonies given from witnesses.

There were similarities here, but most cases were from between eight and fifteen years ago. Had the killer been imprisoned or in hiding for several years?

"Are you feeling okay?" Newton asked, walking into the bullpen from the direction of the garage. "You don't look so good, Beckett." His voice came out gravelly, but at least there was some concern there.

"Just trying to go through these files you pulled. Anything you can direct me to?" As much as I wanted to close all these cold cases, we had one that was still fresh, meaning I'd be able to investigate more than just through pictures.

"No, sorry, girl. Gonzalez and I just found a few dead cats near the city building."

I frowned, not sure what that had to do with a paranormal case. Unless they were paranormals. I needed to remember all animals could be shifters. "Were they similar to the birds?" Anything was possible in this city.

He shook his head. "They had small burn marks but no holes like the birds."

Newton walked over to his desk, sitting in the specially ordered chair that fit his massive width. It had arrived a few days ago after getting stuck somewhere in a huge snowstorm for the holidays. He'd been pretty excited about it.

Burns, but no holes. Was the murderer getting worse? Or did whatever killed the birds right off affect the cats differently?

I opened the next file and sucked in a breath. A body lay on the grass, the heart and stomach a bloody mess.

"What's wrong, Beckett?" Newton asked.

Not sure how to describe it, and with my stomach ready to throw up at the sight of so much blood, I stood, carrying the file over to him.

Newton leaned forward, his eyes needing to be nearly touching the picture to see the minor details. The guy could use some glasses.

"Yeah, that's oddly similar." He leaned back and handed me the file again.

I turned it around to read Alina Young. "She was only eighteen when she died, let's see, three years ago. Do you want to go with me on this one?" I asked.

"Where does it say she's from?" Newton asked, moving his mouse around on the pad. The thing looked miniature in his hands. It was a wonder he didn't break it every time he had to press the button.

I glanced down at the information on the sheet. "Looks like Crescent Ave."

"That's not in the vampire lands, right?" Newton asked. The poor guy had endured the stench of several dead vampires on our last case. He said it was unbearable, even worse than what Tork had mentioned, and I wondered what the difference in smell was between them. I would have thought shifters would have a better sense of smell compared to a guy essentially made from rocks. But what did I know?

I punched the address into the app Tork made us download. Apparently a paranormal had been working to create a map app specifically for Crescent City. Now I just hoped it would work even in the places where I didn't have service, which included like half the city.

A few seconds later, we were en route to an area I'd never been to. From the roads, though, it looked oddly similar to where the cottage was, although not tucked so far back into the woods.

I handed Newton my phone, and after close inspection, he said, "It's in the bruja lands?"

"That's where the address is?" I asked, my voice rising to a higher pitch. I grabbed the phone and studied it again. I'm not sure where I thought it would take me, but to the witches? I wasn't mentally prepared for it.

Newton shrugged. "That's what Tork said one time when we drove past."

Of course, Tork would show Newton all the sections of the city, while leaving me in the dark about the biggest section of my family tree.

"Let's go. It might be good to have backup. I'm not sure how well they'll take to having us snoop around."

"What you mean is they might not like you snooping." Newton gave me a head nod and a knowing smile.

"I doubt they even know I'm part bruja." We walked out into the garage and I went to open my door.

"I'm driving. I won't fit into that soda can you call a car." Newton's face was completely serious.

I laughed, trying to picture him in the passenger seat of

Sonja. Fitting through the door would be the first challenge. A sunroof could help his height, but it might tamper with the structure of the car as it was, and I needed her to last until I'd saved enough to replace her.

"Have you found out any details about your family?" Newton asked, turning down the classical music as he pulled out onto the main street.

I sighed, wishing I could respond with a firm yes. "No. I've been at the, um, library a lot," I lied, barely catching myself before I said something about the cottage in the woods. Heath was the only one who knew anything about it, but I hadn't taken him to see it. "So far I found the dictionary of *tvary* symbols, but that's about it."

Newton nodded, leaning over to see the directions on my phone. He wasn't as close as he usually was with paper. Maybe the screens helped magnify things for him?

"What's your story, Newton? Where were you born?" I might as well use this time to learn more about him.

Before he could answer, he yanked the wheel hard to the right. I glanced around, unable to see what he was trying to dodge but something hit my side of the Hummer. My head slammed back against the seat and the seat belt cut into my neck a bit, but I was alive.

Newton jumped out of the Hummer and stalked around to the side. I rolled the window down a little at a time, unable to move too much since the seat belt was stuck, making it so I couldn't lean forward more than an inch.

"Are you all right, sir? You just ran a stoplight." How he could be so calm and chill when we'd just been hit was beyond me. I detected a slight irritation in his voice, but it was only because we'd been working together for the past couple of weeks. If I could move, I'd probably curse the guy for his driving abilities.

I glanced out the window, the car still next to the door, making it impossible to open. Newton opened the driver door and pulled out the man. His eyes were glazed as if he were in a trance.

"Sir, sir," Newton asked, turning him back and forth and then shaking him a bit. The man looked like an infant compared to the gargoyle. "What's wrong, sir?"

Finally, the man's eyes cleared. "What happened? W-who are you?"

"You hit a Crescent City Police Officer."

The man shook his head, closing and then opening his eyes as if he would see something different after. "I don't remember. What happened?" He glanced around at the surroundings and then back at Newton. "I was on the other side of the city before, but I can't remember anything."

"Where do you live?" I asked from my seat in the Hummer. The sooner we got some answers, the sooner I could get out of this death trap.

"In South Moon. My name is Stanley West and I don't come up this way very often, now that my mother passed."

Newton set the man down, steadying him for a moment on his wobbly legs.

"What did you do before you got into your car?"

"I was packing for a trip to Boston. I called my sister and then stopped at a gas station close to home."

I added all those details to a file in my mind and asked, "Was there anyone around you when you were filling up?"

The man closed his eyes and scrunched his nose, as if it would help him remember what he needed to tell us.

"There was a large truck with a young man, and then a group of bikers filling up. I paid for the fuel with cash and the cashier gave me a strange look, but other than that, those were the only people I came into contact with. That I remember, anyway."

"So, you started driving," Newton said, waving his hand to signal the man should continue.

"I drove down the street that takes me to the roundabout at the south of town, and now I'm here. It's like I blacked out."

Blacked out. Like Nina?

"I'm going to need to take down your information and give you a ticket for reckless endangerment. Will you walk the line for me, please?" Newton motioned to the line at the side of the road.

"I don't drink, and I don't do drugs." The man's voice was more of a plea at this point.

"It's just a quick test," I said, wishing I could unlock my seatbelt and get out to help. "If you don't drink, you'll pass with flying colors."

The man walked along the line, his balance severely impaired, making it difficult to stay there.

Newton leaned over and pushed the car away, looking like he'd just moved a desk rather than a ton of metal. He stopped when it was on the grass next to the road.

"Stanley, we're going to take you into the precinct to ask a few more questions."

Newton opened the back door of his Hummer and basically shoved the man inside, shutting the door with a loud click.

He put the Hummer in reverse and the seatbelt finally loosened enough to be away from the skin on my neck.

"You okay?" Newton asked, turning around and heading back to the precinct. I rubbed the back of my neck and tilted my head from side to side.

"I think so. Just sore is all."

"What do you make of this?" Newton asked, pointing to the man in back.

I glanced back at the man staring through the window. "I'm not sure. We definitely need more answers."

The tingly feeling seeped through me. My sister had experienced blackouts on the other side of the country and now a guy was claiming the same thing? I'd have to ask Nina for more specifics and hope we could connect some detail. Because there had to be a reason people blacked out, right? Or were they just two isolated incidents?

TEN

Booking a human was my least favorite duty as a cop.

Maybe the paranormal division was making me soft since we didn't have the lengthy paperwork to go along with the arrest of a paranormal. And also, I'd had little to do with the two criminals we'd arrested.

I'd been in the hospital for one and Lyra's stay here had been short, two quick days before she'd been moved to a more secure prison. Tork handled that one. Being lunch for a vampire wasn't a life goal of mine, and I figured the shifter in Tork could keep her under control.

Now, Newton had just let me take Stanley West into the precinct, muttering something about staying out of sight of most humans. His bulk would raise eyebrows. He sure hadn't been afraid of itt when he'd pulled Stanley from his vehicle though.

"This guy hit me and another officer while en route to investigate a crime," I told Blaine, the guy closest to the Captain's office.

"Why were you investigating anything?" the man asked,

scowling at me. "Do you think escaping the records room on a ride-along will help get you back upstairs?"

Anger coursed through me and it was all I could do to keep my composure.

"I don't think you're the one with the authority here. Give us a room to talk and tell the Captain where I am."

Instead of waiting for him to budge, I steered Stanley toward the interrogation room I'd used a few weeks ago. I'd met with Evelyn, a sketch artist, about a potential killer. We'd figured out he was just a lovesick guy who'd fallen for the wrong girl.

As I thought of Evelyn, I wondered if she might have some insight into the blackout thing. She was a diviner, part of the Elemental group, and could see things with a decent description. If I couldn't get any information from this guy and Nina, maybe she'd help.

I sat Stanley down, grateful he hadn't put up a fight. I think he was nervous about losing time and what he might have done in the meantime. It was the same fear I'd seen on Nina's face when she talked about it. Hours going by without an idea what I'd done or where I'd gone? Yeah, I'd be freaked out about it too.

"Let's go over your day, Stanley," I said, taking a seat across the table.

"I already told you. I packed, talked to my sister, and then went to get gas. The next thing I knew, I woke up dangling from a guy who could fight the Hulk on the opposite side of town."

I leaned over the table. "What time did all this take place?"

Stanley stared at the table as if it was playing a recap of what he'd done that day. "I wanted to get on the road after the morning traffic, but before it got too late. By the time I'd packed, it was probably nine. Getting gas would've been ten or fifteen minutes later."

It was three o'clock when we picked him up. He had no idea what he'd done for six hours?

"Do you like animals?" He frowned, looking as though he didn't understand my line of thinking.

He shrugged. "I have two dogs. Why?"

"What are your thoughts on birds? Cats?" I drummed my fingers along the tabletop, waiting for his answer.

A knock came at the door and I turned, wondering if it was the Captain already. "Come in."

Tork appeared instead, his general mood nonplussed. "Head back down to the, um, records room, Beckett. Newton will meet you there."

I didn't move, not wanting to give up a chance to figure out what was going on with my sister and this man, or if the two things were even connected.

"I'm fine. We're just having a brief chat, aren't we, Stanley?" I turned back to the man, who trembled on the other side of the table. "Okay, we're not that scary and we probably won't press charges. We just want answers."

"Beckett," Tork growled, a warning tone edging the word.

I shoved out of the chair and gritted my teeth, keeping my voice low so I could talk to Tork without Stanley hearing too much. "What could be so important that I need to go down right now? Can't I watch you interrogate this witness?"

Instead of speaking, he yanked on my arm and pulled me out of the room.

"I need you to follow up on the case you were looking into," Tork said, his voice low. He glanced around, making sure no one was close and then looked back at me. "Something's happening with the animals in this town. Gonzalez called in several squirrels with the exact holes we've seen in the birds and cats. We don't need the humans to catch wind of this."

I had an official assignment. A strange one, but at least it was something. And the idea of heading out to the bruja coven made the pull away that much easier.

"For the record, my half-sister has been having blackouts as well. I know, it's a long shot, but it's worth trying to see if there's something in common."

"Didn't she fly back to California?" Tork asked, leaning against the door to the interrogation room.

"No, she's staying at my apartment for a while. But I just wanted to keep you informed of it."

Tork smiled, the action genuine. "It's about time you told me first before asking forgiveness. I'll let you know of anything I find out from this. Head out now. We don't want things to get worse."

I took a step closer, wishing we were in our own bullpen and could speak freely. "Do you think it connects to the Shadowmoon Coven?"

"With the pictures Gonzalez sent me of the squirrels and the pictures of the girl on your desk, I'd say there is some connection between the two. At least whoever killed her is only killing animals."

"What if they escalate and start using humans? Or larger shifters?" I said, driving the point home with a look of disgust.

Tork didn't seem like he wanted to continue this conversation in the open. "Go, I'll handle this."

Instead of walking through the door in the closet of the break room, I opted for the front door.

"Newton," I said, when he picked up the phone. "Let's try this again."

ELEVEN

I'd never believed the hype that Hummers were indestructible but based on the way Stanley's car had left only a scratch in the paint on the passenger door, I was impressed.

We took a different route this time, watching out for any cars that might come barreling through stop lights and signs.

As we arrived closer to the bruja lands, the tingly feeling crept through me. I thought of all the people who lived there, faceless witches and warlocks. There could be family there, my family. But as my excitement rose to the fact I might find bruja who could tell me something, anything about my mother, Lee Vance's words cycled back through.

Maybe I didn't value something like the bruja did, but an all-out war starting because of a stolen book sounded ludicrous to me.

What were the bruja going to do? Throw me out because I was a police officer? Or because I was Belinda Sanchez's daughter?

Then again, only a few people knew it. But would they recognize me like Adelaide had in the grocery store?

These were all questions I couldn't worry about. I was here to do my job and get answers. Newton at my side through this would help as well. Not many people wanted to mess with the solid mass of rock and hopefully, the evidence we uncovered would lead to justice for Alina Young.

There were several old houses all in a row, vines nearly covering the outsides and the trees surrounding them made it look almost dark, even though it was early afternoon.

I walked to the front gate of the house and pushed, thinking the gate would open automatically.

Nothing.

There wasn't a latch or any way of opening the iron wall.

"Hello?" I called. I wished I was back in the vampire lands. At least they believed in landscaping and I could see the sun in the heat of the day.

"Hello? I'm Detective Claire Beckett. I've come to ask some questions about the death of Alina Young." I said it as loud as I could, even cupping my hands around my mouth to amplify the sound the distance of thirty feet to the front door.

Stillness met my listening ear, and I wasn't sure what to do. How did I learn about things without people to question?

Newton lumbered up the path, having found a parking spot down the road. He probably double-parked.

"There's no way to get in through the gate to even knock." I waved at the black iron bars, frustrated for more than a girl's dead body. It was like they were shutting me out as well, for something I didn't do and still didn't have the full knowledge of. Irrational, I know, but those were the thoughts that ran through my brain right then.

"These kinds of gates have a different mechanism keeping them closed," Newton said, inspecting the hinge.

"Really? What is it?"

Before he answered, his fist went slamming into the gate,

sending it flying off both hinges. It landed in the tall grass to the side of the walkway.

"Well, that's one way to do it," I said, chuckling. For someone who was very by-the-book, this seemed like a stretch from Newton, but one I was okay with. I needed some answers to help this young girl's memory and stop the other animal killings. Hopefully I'd find Sloan in the process, or any of the bruja who might give me answers.

We walked up to the door and knocked. It opened after I'd barely placed my knuckles on it. I jumped back, my heart racing as an older woman stepped out.

"Yes?" she asked, her lips forming a tight line.

"We're here to investigate a cold case in our database. Alina Young, killed three years ago."

The grim look changed to sadness, and the woman stepped back, waving us through to enter the house.

A wave of indecision hit me and I wondered if this was like walking into a vampire's lair with a paper cut. Would I make it out alive?

Newton gave me a push and I stumbled forward, catching myself before I catapulted down to the front stoop.

"Careful," I hissed, not looking back at him completely.

My anger had surged at being made to look like a fool, but I had to remember Newton was just stronger than he probably thought.

The woman led us into a small room complete with couch and chairs, the brown floral fabric on them reminding me of the old school television shows.

"Please sit here," she said, wiping at the corner of her eye. I was going to guess she was Alina's mother.

"Cindy, please bring our guests some tea," she called up the stairs.

"No need for that, ma'am," I said, stuttering a bit on the last word. And from the way Newton looked at the furniture in the room, it was best if we kept standing and made this all about the question-and-answer session.

"We just have a few questions and we'll be on our way." I waited, studying her face for approval. She blinked several times and nodded. "Can you tell us about Alina? Who did she hang out with before her death? Was there anything that warned you about danger?"

The woman sat down in the chair, more likely fell into it, looking like she'd been carrying a heavy load and her legs could no longer support her.

"My name is Mary Michaels Young. Alina was my oldest child. Very gifted with magic. She spent many evenings with a group of our coven, honing her skills and working to become a strong bruja."

Sobs choked her words and I shifted from one foot to the other, uncomfortable with the scene. I wasn't the best at comforting people, and a complete stranger in tears only added to the stress. But as a detective, I needed to make sure I knew the facts, and if the woman needed to cry through it, I could handle it.

"Who was in this group?" I asked, trying to keep my voice as soothing and calm as possible.

"There were several girls her age. Truvy, Alora, Sands, Ilo, Laureth. They'd worked together for so long it was just normal to see the six of them huddled in a group. But things slowly changed over the weeks preceding Alina's death. The girls were more distant, from us and from each other."

"They weren't talking to one another? What changed?"

The woman shook her head, tears forming even more now. She swallowed with effort. It was difficult to see, but the best way to comfort her was to find her daughter's killer.

"We don't know. Alina barely ate, barely slept. It was like she was a walking zombie."

I thought it out, hoping to connect the pieces or at least find the questions that could do so.

"Why do you think Alina was the only one killed?" Then remembering I hadn't gotten the information, I said, "What happened to the other girls?"

"They were found miles away, tied up in the shifter lands. If you want to search for who might have killed my beautiful girl, you'll search there." Mary Michaels's lips pursed and her jaw tightened, looking much stronger than when we'd first come to the house.

I forced a smile, not sure I wanted to go accusing the shifters of problems. It never went well, especially under Heath's watch.

A girl appeared at the top of the stairs, her dark brown hair braided over one shoulder. She hurried down when she saw us and sat in a small chair next to Mary.

"Cindy, these are detectives from the police department to ask about Alina." Mary glanced down at her and the young woman nodded.

"Hi," she said, nodding at us.

"She's our middle daughter," Mary said, giving her a kiss on the top of her head. "She's been through a lot, ever since Alina died."

I squatted down, trying to gain her trust. Cindy finally looked up, her eyes narrowed in on me.

"How old are you, Cindy?" I asked, standing again. She might have looked a lot younger when I first glimpsed her, but she was no child.

"Eighteen."

"We've found several animals with injuries just like hers over the past few days, and we hope to find some answers so we can bring her killer to justice. Can you tell us anything about your sister's death?"

The girl's expression tightened. Her voice broke when she said, "Alina wouldn't talk to me before she died. We'd always been close and she'd always helped me with things, especially magic." A tear rolled down her cheek, and I could see the pain in her eyes.

I pictured this new relationship Nina and I were building. Not quite the same thing, but it would be hard to be cut off completely, especially when living in the same house.

"Where can I find these other girls?" Stick with the facts, not the emotions of the women. It was the best way to get justice. I'd already learned emotions didn't always play out with a clear head and the correct answer.

"They don't talk to anyone right now," Mary said, wiping a handkerchief under one eye.

"It's been three years, right?" Newton asked. I'd almost forgotten he was here since he'd been so quiet. "They haven't spoken to anyone since?"

Mary shook her head, twisting the handkerchief in her hands. "Not that I know for sure, but it's what I've been told. We haven't been to a coven council since Alina's death."

I took a step forward, sinking down so I could be more at eye-level with her. "What is the coven council? Who all takes part in it?"

"There are several of the higher bruja families, bruja nobles is what most call them. They make up the governing council of the Shadowmoon coven. They set Council meetings for Tuesday evenings. Don't show up, and you're threatened to be kicked out of the coven."

"And yet, you live here, right next to them, and don't attend?"

"We have nowhere else to go," the woman sobbed. I'd

known that feeling, trapped and unable to do anything about it. It had been my life under Nina's guardianship until I'd been old enough to graduate, attend college, and then join the police academy. The stifling protection, the demands to do exactly as told. Maybe that's why I struggled with authority to some degree.

"Thank you for your time," I said, realizing we wouldn't get much more. Mary had devolved into deeper sobs and I knew the best plan for me was to find out who had killed her daughter, hopefully giving her some closure about the whole thing. The sister seemed to have answers, I'd just have to get her away from her mother and ask those more in-depth questions.

"We will be sure to let you know as soon as we've found anything," Newton said, stepping out the door.

Mary stood and followed us. She swiped at the fresh tears falling down her cheeks and asked, "Why now? Why the sudden interest in my daughter's case?"

"Because we have the Paranormal Division, ma'am, and we're hoping to get our cold cases solved." A sharp pain jabbed at my forehead, and I flinched back, trying not to react to it. I wasn't immune to headaches, but the intensity and sharpness of it was more than I'd experienced before.

"Thank you so much. We've felt the hole from her absence, but we've tried to move forward."

"Where was the body found?" Newton asked, stepping outside and onto the porch. How he had even fit through the door was a question in itself.

Mary pointed to the east. "Three blocks down and the first street over. But you can't go much further into the courtyard without being invited."

That piqued my interest. "How does someone get an invitation?"

The woman's eyes grew wide, and she bit her bottom lip.

As if trying to come up with the words, she said, "You really don't want an invitation. Outsiders aren't allowed back out in most cases."

I'd like to see them try.

As we walked back to the Hummer, I turned to Newton and asked, "Why did you want to know where she was killed?"

"To give you the chance to find your special symbols. They've helped in the past. Why not look for them now?"

I smiled at him, grateful because my ability was helping to aid in solving cases. At least I hadn't lost it completely. I just needed to figure out the rest of my abilities so I could use them to stop the pain of women like that.

WE DROVE to the spot Mary had designated and got out to search for any clues. It had been three years since her death, but I wasn't sure how long the *tvary* symbols lasted, or if some other magic had wiped them away. I'd been able to see symbols at the crime scene of my mother's murder eight years later. So it was something.

"What is it you see when you find these symbols?" Newton asked, walking next to me more for moral support than anything.

I pulled out my notebook and handed it to him. "I'm not the best artist, but those are about what I see. They come in different colors, which I've learned are signs of the killer's strength."

I turned back to the ground near the corner of the street, glancing at one picture from the file to get a better read on the location.

In the upper right corner of the picture, there was what looked like a small bush. I stood up and glanced around the block. I was on the wrong corner. There, just across the street, was a bush that matched.

"We need to look over here." I took off, the street nearly empty except for the row of houses on either side.

I did a long inspection of the ground, feeling the pressure as the seconds continued to build, finding no sign of the *tvary*. If *tvary* could remain, I concluded this was not the scene of the crime. Another stab of pain hit me, only this time it didn't go away as quickly.

"It wasn't here," I said, holding my forehead. The pain was so intense I was finding it difficult to breathe normally.

"What do you mean it wasn't here? That's exactly how it looks in the picture," Newton said, holding up the photo for me.

"I'm saying there are no *tvary* in this area. She must have been killed somewhere else."

I widened my search, keeping one eye open to focus despite the pain, hoping maybe I'd missed a symbol in the process. It was always possible for her to have been killed somewhere else. There had been dozens of victims in the 27th precinct who'd been found in one spot, but the act of murder, or attempted murder, had taken place somewhere else. Maybe that had happened to Alina and her body had been left on this corner.

After several more minutes, there was still nothing. My headache had increased to the point I couldn't think clearly.

"Let's head back to the precinct. We need to get more information on Alina's friends and past. Maybe then we'll find more clues." I turned, walking toward the Hummer, with Newton on my heels. And I needed pain medication before I wanted to take a hammer to my skull.

"If it's a cold case, what would we be able to find in the system? Tork said something about the bruja coven not being open with their internal problems."

It was a valid question, but I wasn't in the mood. I wanted to knock my head up against a brick wall just to have the pain behind my eyes ease up. The lack of *tvary* always made me anxious, and I had to do something to get my stomach to loosen up.

"Maybe there are other cases we can connect to it. We just need to find something."

"I already did that. We pulled every file remotely close to this case."

With a few minor hits of my fist against my forehead, I started walking back toward the Hummer. I couldn't walk straight, let alone think of the details clearly enough to solve this case.

When Newton didn't question me further, I was more than grateful, needing the silence to think through the answers we already had.

If I'd learned anything from the few interactions with the bruja coven, it was that I needed to tread carefully before charging in and accusing anyone without solid evidence to back it up. It was a lesson Heath refused to let me forget. From all my interactions with the other groups and packs in Crescent City, I'd bet they wouldn't take kindly to it either.

TWELVE

Researching at the precinct was always an adventure, but I hoped with the new programs I'd be able to find something to help get this case moving again. Newton had pulled out a bottle of ibuprofen once we'd gotten back to the Hummer, and my headache was easing as we approached the precinct.

"Did you eat something different?" he asked. He'd already fired at least a dozen questions at me, and even though I was grateful, I needed him to stop talking so my brain could just relax for a moment.

He'd finally left to get me a coffee from the place around the corner while I entered the search parameters of death with holes, not really knowing what else to put. Then I added the names of Alina's friends. Fifteen results popped up. It could've been worse; we'd worked with fifty and sixty files on the past two cases I'd been on. As I clicked through, though, I realized these were all news articles from the online paranormal newspaper. Not much information there.

"What are you working on?" Tork asked, crunching on something behind me. I turned to find him holding a regular bag of chips. He usually ate something with meat in it, so it surprised me to see this was just regular cheddar and sour cream.

"Trying to find things to go along with the cold case we found. We have some files, but there have to be more closely tied to Alina's case. The others Newton pulled didn't match exactly. Have you had to work with the Shadowmoon Coven much?"

"Not if I can help it," Tork said. "Trying to get through to their heads is like trying to drill through a cement wall using a spoon."

"What's the girl's last name again?" Gonzalez asked, walking over to my desk from the garage.

"Michaels or Young," I said, watching to see if he had any reaction to that.

"Like your new friend, Sloan." Tork pointed toward me and I frowned.

Why hadn't anyone mentioned it before? "That's Sloan's last name?"

The headache had subsided, but I was worried if I moved wrong, it would come back in full force. I rubbed at my temples and along my eyebrow bone, hoping to keep it away for longer.

Was I too stressed? No, since we'd had little going on for a few weeks. This case was already a lot less work than previous ones.

"What the hell's wrong with you?" Tork asked.

"Just a little headache," I said, heading straight for my desk.

"It wasn't just a headache," Newton said, coming up behind me. "You crouched down in pain, looking like you wanted to die."

I growled, not wanting to tip off Tork about all the things I just experienced. I've never had that feeling and wasn't sure what had caused it. It wasn't like I had used extra power because of the *tvary*. There had been none.

"Beckett, is this part of your treatment?" Tork asked.

I bristled, angry he even knew about it. "What do you mean by treatment?"

Him knowing about my therapy was not helping the situation, and with the ache in my forehead, I wanted to punch him.

"Your visits to Dr. Stringer. Have you talked to her about headaches?"

"This is my second one since I've arrived in Crescent City. I don't think it's anything she needs to know about."

I wished he would just let it drop, but he was a detective and it seemed like our personalities were meant for this job, never knowing when to quit researching or investigating something.

"Give her a call," Tork said. "She does a good job." I turned toward him.

"Wait, you've gone to see her?" I glanced at Gonzalez, who didn't look fazed by our conversation.

Tork let out a laugh. "Of course I have. When you're the only member of the Paranormal Division in Crescent City, you have to go through all the shit by yourself. Which means I've spent many hours sitting in her office talking about a bit of everything."

"I've met with her too," Gonzalez said. "She knows her stuff."

"Does she know you're both shifters?" I asked, glancing between the two of them.

Both Tork and Gonzalez started laughing. Once they finally settled down, Tork said, "She's an earth elemental. That's why Captain Woods sends us to her. She's good at the soothing properties to help you figure out how to change things."

Mind blown.

It wasn't often I was this shocked about anything, since I expected the weird here, but now I wanted to go to her office just to figure out if she gave off any clues.

She'd mentioned nothing about me being paranormal, which is what most did when they met me. To be honest, most of them stared at me like I was some strange animal because I must not give off a distinct signal to what I am. It made me wonder if Stephanie Carter, the gal we'd questioned along with her brother, Levi, during the vampire investigation, got the same looks. Then again, she knew she was half-shifter, half-bruja.

At least I wasn't the only one in the precinct who saw Dr. Stringer.

"I'm supposed to have a meeting with her tomorrow." I glanced at my calendar. "I'll just ask about it then."

Tork shrugged. "Suit yourself. Just remember it's okay to need her help."

I smirked. "You sound like you could be in a commercial for her business."

"I'd be up for it. That's how much she's helped me." Tork was full of surprises, but what I was coming to see was instead of hiding weakness like most did at the 27th precinct, Gonzalez and Tork made it natural. And even though it had been several weeks, my anxiety level about Lee Vance reappearing was still off the charts. Helping that would be a miracle, indeed.

I turned back to my desk, waiting for the screen to appear as I moved the mouse around a few times.

"What did you find out about the cold case?" Tork asked from his desk.

I waited for Newton to take the lead on that one. "We got there, and the woman told us where her body was found.

Claire couldn't find any of the *tvary* and then she was basically crippled with a headache."

"Thanks, Newton," I said, rolling my eyes.

"He's telling me everything," Tork said, eyebrows raised like Newton had just won a big prize for honesty.

Shaking off the comment, I said, "We got the names of five other girls who Alina hung out with. But in the couple of weeks before her death, something put distance between them. Maybe if we find more about the friends, we'll be able to understand what they were doing and why the sudden change."

Newton piped in. "The mom said the girls were pretty much inseparable, always practicing magic, and then suddenly, about two or three weeks before Alina's death, they stopped talking and hanging out together."

"They stopped hanging out with Alina? Or everyone stopped hanging out together?"

"From what we gathered," I said, opening the database where we could search for different citizens and species, "they all stopped hanging out with each other."

"So then why was Alina the only dead girl out of the group? Why none of the others?" Tork folded his arms over his chest, looking like he was trying to reason through it with us.

I had no answer, since Mary hadn't known either. It was a hope that in searching for the names of the other girls, we could piece a few more clues together. I held up the file with a line of information in it and said, "Is this really the only information we have on her murder?"

"As far as I know," Tork nodded. "This murder happened before I was down here."

I glanced down at the sheet and saw the names Murray and Fielding. "Are these detectives still with the precinct?"

Tork walked over and looked where my finger was pointing. "Murray retired. Fielding just transferred to one of the other divisions outside of town."

"Does it happen a lot?" I asked. There seemed to be a lot of turnover in Crescent City, especially among the humans. I thought of Zach, the coroner before Stacia. It was better she was in there now so we could get actual answers instead of not understanding the situation or what animal might have caused a bite or mark on a victim.

"Must be hard trying to convince them they're not crazy if they see anything out of the ordinary," I said. It had taken a bit to adjust for me, even, and I'd already started seeing the *tvary* before I arrived here.

"Yeah," Tork said, sitting back at his desk. "It's usually that their counterparts don't appreciate living here."

I'd only been here over two and a half months, but this place was better than anywhere I'd ever lived. It was almost like a dream but also had its drawbacks. Learning I was secretly a witch for most of my life didn't always sit well, especially since I didn't know the extent of my powers just yet.

"Okay, so should we split up and question the detectives?" Newton asked, always the voice of reason, pulling us back to the task.

"I can go talk to the detective," I said, jumping at the chance to find some more evidence for this case.

Tork shook his head. "I'll take it. I already need to speak to someone about that domestic violence case."

When he mentioned it, my mind went back to the guy we'd picked up earlier. "Did you figure out what was causing the blackouts for Stanley?"

Again, Tork shook his head. "He remembers nothing. Maybe you should ask your sister some more questions? It could be a better way to corroborate their stories, if they were connected in some way. Why don't you do that after researching the girls? There has to be some information in the database." He smirked at me, our inside joke coming up yet again.

"Is there a way to just go onto the bruja lands and ask?" Look at me getting out of the typical and volunteering for bruja duty.

Tork's eyes narrowed, his teeth bared, sending a zip of fear running through me. "Are you willing to die for it?"

I let out a nervous laugh. "It's not like I'm going to go accusing anyone."

It was a lame defense, but a part of me hoped I'd find a thread of my own once I was there. Maybe even find Sloan.

"It's better to wait for the bruja to come to us."

Frustration pressed into my chest, and I shook my head. "That's how this girl's murder turned into a cold case, Tork." I practically spat at him, annoyed with his relaxed tactics once again. But he had more experience with the different species in Crescent City, and I just had to find a way as soon as possible to get the information I needed. "I'm sorry, but the recent murders need justice as well, before the killer strikes again."

"I know you want to close this case, Beckett," Tork said, his voice much cooler than it usually was. "But I'm recommending we wait a day or two before we charge in there, guns blazing."

The truth of his words hit me in the chest. Everyone needed balance and although I wanted answers for a lot of things, playing it safe might just be worth it. "Fine. I'll let you know as soon as I find anything on the girls."

The guys left and the bullpen was eerily silent. I spent the next thirty minutes looking up every possible name and combination in the database, but again, true to the fashion of the paranormal community, I only had first names. The other great thing was the oddness of the names. Truvy, Alora, Sands, Ilo,

Laureth. There weren't any humans listed in Crescent City with them.

I read through the story from the paranormal newspaper about the day they were found in the shifter lands. I'd have to ask Heath about it the next time I spoke with him. He'd have an opinion on it for sure.

I decided to knock off and head home. Between the adrenaline from the accident and the exhaustion from the intense headache, I needed time to relax. That was usually when I locked onto some ideas I couldn't see when constantly looking for them.

Something caused my focus to sharpen once I got out to the garage. I thought I saw a shadow duck behind one of the cement pillars. With my keys positioned between my fingers, I put myself in a defensive stance, ready for whatever was lurking in the darkness.

"Hello?" My pulse quickened, and I tried to push away the pictures of Lee Vance preparing to attack me. Maybe I should've been more focused on his case than this girl's, but we had fresh evidence for her. She deserved justice, and I was a big girl, even though most of me wanted to rush back into the precinct and wait this out.

I jumped into the driver's seat after over a minute of watching and listening. My nerves were frayed, and I was grateful the drive home was quick. At least no one had followed me this time.

When I walked in the door, the smell of spices and rice hit me. Definitely not something I was used to when coming home from work. Another reason this new relationship with my sister had its perks.

"Hey Nina," I said, dropping my things next to the door. "Smells good."

She turned around, grinning at me. "I learned a few things in California."

Nina had never been much of a cook. Then again, neither had our mother. We'd grown up on breakfast for dinner and takeout for the most part.

I walked over to the kitchen and leaned over to look into the pot, the orange sauce bubbling. "Tikka Masala?"

She nodded, adding a few shakes of salt. "Yeah, I learned to make it from the lady next door. She was always creating these fancy meals, and they smelled so good, like she'd lifted them up next to the air vent so I would smell them when I was home from work. She taught me here and there, and at the time, I figured I could use it to impress Brad."

Tears welled up in her eyes and, even though I was still awkward about comforting people, there was no better time than now to start, especially with my half-sister.

I wrapped my arms around her shoulders and pulled her in for a hug, letting her sob against me.

"It's all right, Nina," I said, awkwardly patting her head. "You'll find the right guy."

"I don't know," Nina said. She pulled back a bit and sniffed, using the back of her hand to wipe at a stray tear. "It's hard enough as it is to find someone when you're in journalism and the crazy hours I had to keep. But someone who can put up with all the baggage I'm coming with? Never knowing my father, raising my half-sister after our mother died. Who's going to take on that role?"

I chuckled. "At least you acknowledge the baggage."

She threw me a quick scowl and then laughed. "We're quite a pair, aren't we?"

A thought struck me and I asked, "You never met your dad?"

Guilt coursed through me I'd never cared enough to ask,

but it seemed Nina was ready to talk about almost anything tonight.

"I think I saw a picture of him once," Nina said, pouring herself a glass of wine. After a sip, she said, "What about you?"

I tried to remember, and it was almost like a hazy picture in my mind. "You would probably know him better than I would," I said. She was four years older than me, so she'd been six when he'd left. "Do you know his name?"

Leaning up against the counter, Nina shook her head. "I don't remember it, but he was always so nice, from what I can remember."

"Why do you think Mom got rid of the guys?" My mom had kept a lot of things from me, but she would've at least told me if my father was dead, right?

Nina stared at the ceiling for several moments before saying, "I think Mom had a lot going on she couldn't share."

"Do you think our dads are out there?"

Nina shrugged. "Probably, but I'm not in a hurry to go looking for mine. If he'd really wanted to be in my life, he would've worked harder to find me." There was the arrogant bitch attitude I was used to.

As I thought about the bruja coven, about the tightness of security, how had my mom escaped? Or had it not been as bad back when she'd left? For the thousandth time, Lee Vance's words about my mother betraying the coven looped through my mind. Had she caused the distrust among the coven?

Picturing the cottage house and everything stored inside it, I could only imagine how well she'd prepared for whatever danger was coming.

"Did Mom have any sons?" I asked, remembering the comment Heath made about me having a brother. That was back when I first got here, and I'd forgotten about it until now.

There had been no evidence of a male sibling at the cottage, but it was still a possibility.

Nina shook her head, scrunching up her nose like that was the biggest load of shit she'd heard in a while. I took it as either we didn't have one, or she didn't know about him.

"We had a guy who drove his car into us today," I said, trying to segue over to ask her more questions about her blackouts.

"He ran into a police cruiser? That's probably the dumbest move he could've made." Nina stood back up and turned off the stove.

I opened my mouth, ready to tell her it was actually a Hummer, and then remembered she didn't need to know all the details of my life. At least not yet. Maybe once she'd learned more about the paranormal world.

"We're just waiting for the rice to finish and then we can eat."

I nodded. "The man claims to not remember driving to that part of town. He started in the South end, and where he hit us was in the north. He'd planned a trip to head out of town, which is south."

Nina sat down, never taking her eyes from me as she took another sip of wine.

"That's kind of how things happen with me," she said, her eyes looking a little more frightened than usual. "I would head out for work and then suddenly I would be across town, at the same location every time. That's why I was late so many times in a row."

"Did you ever investigate what you might have done during that time?" I leaned over the table, hoping to get some snippet of information from her that would help us.

"Of course," Nina said, sliding a plate with rice and chicken tikka masala piled on top. She even had some naan bread from a package, but it was better than sandwich bread. "But every time, I would end up on the same street, almost exactly the same parking spot."

Did it mean she'd been hypnotized at some point and directed to go there? Or were there forces trying to get her to acknowledge her past?

"Did you ever have to report on people or animals dying with holes in their chest and abdomen?" There were so many things to unwrap from what Nina was going through, and I just hoped we'd get to the bottom of her problems before anyone got hurt. And if I could connect her situation to my current case in any way would be a bonus.

Again, with the expression of disbelief. "Claire, I reported a lot of homicides in California, mostly gunshot victims. That meant there were usually holes in those sections."

I nodded, taking a bite of the food. It was actually edible.

We ate in silence for some time, and I thought about what she'd said. These holes were definitely not from gunshot wounds, unless it was like the vampire-hunter gun sized up another hundred millimeters.

But they didn't look like gunshot wounds, not in the chest of the bird shifter boy or from the pictures I'd seen of Alina.

What magic would be used on bruja and shifters alike? And who would target them?

THIRTEEN

I prepared to leave early the next morning, first for my appointment with Dr. Stringer and then to work, when I spotted Heath sitting in his car right next to Sonja.

"What are you doing here this early?" I asked. "Don't you have some duties as mayor to take care of?" I'd asked him occasionally, mostly because I wasn't sure what he had to do as mayor besides attend meetings. And it seemed like he was always popping up at the strangest times.

"And miss the look on your *cheerful* face this early in the morning? It's priceless." He gave me a cockeyed grin, sending my stomach into gymnastic twists.

Don't smile. Don't smile.

Damn it.

I kept the smile low key and said, "Some of us don't do well with mornings, no matter how many years we've had to get up early."

"I just wanted to check in and make sure you're alright," he said, leaning his elbow on his door as he glanced down at his shoes. At least the weather had warmed up some, but there was still snow on the ground and I shivered a bit as I stared at him.

His words seemed to strike an odd chord in my chest and I asked, "What do you mean if I'm alright? You're my protector, shouldn't you know everything that's going on in my life? Wait, you usually know it before I do."

"Well, I know quite a bit, but you have your moments of surprise," he said, looking more serious than I was comfortable with. "I was actually more curious about what happened yesterday. Tork told me you had some headache when you were on bruja lands?"

I groaned. I'd expected Tork to tell Captain Woods about the headache, but I hadn't thought he'd go blabbing it to Heath. But I could see Heath needing to know what to watch for, being my protector and all.

"It was nothing," I said, giving a quick shrug. "I just took a couple of ibuprofen and went back to work." True, in a sense, but I still wasn't back to my normal self, energy-wise. Night-mares do love lack of sleep.

"Claire Beckett: always the diligent officer." I expected his words to be sarcastic, but they had a sort of reverence to the tone.

"Is there anything else you need?" I asked, not wanting things to get weird. We'd settled into this strange middle place, where we weren't enemies, but the tension between us seemed to heighten each time he was around. That could just be from me over analyzing everything. Falling for the city's mayor and my protector was not a cliché I would fall into.

Ah, who was I kidding. I thought he was hot. It didn't mean marriage or even an intimate relationship was in the cards. Especially with my track record of men. I hadn't found a guy yet who interested me more than my job, which meant the guys eventually got sick of coming in second.

"No, it's been a couple of days, and I wanted to check in with you." A quick look of guilt passed over his face and I knew something was wrong.

"Did you find out something?" I had left the question open-ended, hoping to bait him into spilling whatever secrets he had that concerned me.

"Why would you ask that?"

"Because I've seen the look on your face enough to know you're hiding something from me."

Heath turned his gaze to the front windshield, then let out a deep breath. "Some of the PFBI found evidence of Lee Vance in Boston."

The news hit me like a rock wall, the way I imagined Newton's fist would feel to whatever object it slammed into. I took a step back, trying to let my brain process this.

If he was in Boston, he wasn't here.

The person I thought had been stalking me, was not the shapeshifter who took over my dreams.

"Where did they find him? What was the evidence?" My detective brain clicked on and I wanted to know all the facts so I could put the final pieces together.

Heath's phone rang, and he glanced at it before pressing the button to silence it. "He was in your old apartment," he said, staring at me with more intensity than I'd seen in a long time.

"Wait, what? He was staying in my apartment, the one I shared with Tori?"

He nodded, no hint of a smile on his face.

"How did they catch him?"

"They didn't. He was gone by the time the police pulled up. One of your old neighbors called it in after sensing something wasn't right. Captain Southwick is the one who informed me."

My old boss. At least he wasn't completely against me, although he had good reason to be. I'd disobeyed his order not to investigate by breaking into the morgue to get a look at Tori's autopsy.

"Does the Captain know Lee Vance is a shapeshifter? Does he know anything about the paranormal world?"

Heath shook his head and said, "We sent him information, just like we would on any other case, describing the suspect and that he might be after information about you."

Not knowing how to react to all this, I lifted my keys and glanced at my watch. "Shit, I need to go. I'm going to be late."

I got into the car and turned the key, but the engine didn't turn over. I tried again and again, hoping I could drive away and let my brain and my nervous system process this.

When coaxing didn't start the car, I breathed out a sigh and opened the driver's door. Walking over to Heath, I said, "I'm going to need a ride today."

"Hop in." Not that I needed to spend any more time with him in confined quarters when my emotions and feelings for him were on a constant rollercoaster, but it was nice to have a backup plan so I wouldn't arrive late to my appointment.

Heath drove to Dr. Stringer's office without saying much. I was grateful for that, since I was still trying to process the psycho escaped convict who'd been squatting in my old apartment. I tried to think of anything he could've found, knowing I'd brought all of my belongings with me when I'd moved here. Tori's family had been dispatched to come get her things, but had they left anything I'd forgotten?

Heath parked in front of Dr. Stringer's office and turned to me. "I don't know how to tell you this," he said, his expression showing more concern than I'd ever seen it.

What could be worse than the nightmare of my life studying where I used to live? The thought of it sent chills of fear through me. "There was a break-in at your storage shed. There is no video evidence of who did it, but I think we know. You have something Lee Vance wants, and we need to figure out what it is before he gets to you."

I opened and closed my mouth, feeling like a fish out of water. "He wants the Codex," I said, breathing shallowly to keep from screaming. "But I don't know what it looks like or if I even have it."

Several moments passed between us, my brain skipping from possible scenario to the next. I'd looked through several of the bookshelves at my mother's cottage, hoping to find something that referred to the Codex or that even said, "Codex."

Nothing.

Maybe I was thinking of it all wrong. I kept picturing this giant book, with a worn cover and old buckles with a strap to keep it closed. Could it be smaller than that?

"When are you off?"

"Saturday," I said.

"We should probably go through all your boxes in the storage shed then. Maybe if Nina is still here, she can find whatever it is she's been dreaming about."

"You want me to invite my sister to the shifter lands?"

I didn't know whether to be annoyed or angry at the idea.

"It's not that big of a deal if she's there," he said, his tone sharp. "I just think if we're going to go through your mother's belongings, it might be best for us to do it together. Less work? Maybe you can figure out who or what brought her here to Crescent City."

"You mean back to Boston, because that's where she went."

He sighed and said, "I don't know how all this fits together. I promise I'm not a seer and I don't have all knowledge of the paranormal world. But I know when it comes to your family,

Beckett, nothing is a coincidence. Are you sure you know nothing about what your mother did?"

I was ready to laugh in his face at that thought. He knew I barely understood what my mother's "real" life looked like, and even after weeks of combing through her books, I'd found little besides the travelogue.

"I should ask you that question. Are you sure you know nothing more about my mother than what you've told me?" I was going to be late to my appointment, but I'd finally called Heath out, and I hoped he wouldn't evade the question this time.

"I'd only heard of your mother. I saw her once when I was a pup. She'd come to our house, frantic about something I didn't understand, then begged to speak with my father, who was away in the far parts of the shifter lands trying to fix something. She didn't stay, saying there were lives at stake. But as a five-year-old wolf-pup, the danger could've been from anything."

My brain called up the memory of the two letters in Heath's desk drawer. I'd found them when I'd ordered a search of his house. They'd both been addressed to Heath, which was also the name of the current mayor's father. I'd read the first, but something about how close the date was to my mother's death had scared me. Yeah, not my finest moment as a detective.

I had to know now. "What does the second letter say?"

"Are you sure you want to know?" I nodded, and he slipped his hand into his jacket pocket and pulled out his phone. After a couple of swipes, he handed it to me. There on the screen was a letter written in my mother's handwriting.

HEATH,

It's not going well. I need you to meet me in Boston to take ownership of this. Shadowmoon Coven are after me and the Black Order has gone dark. I need to get rid of this. My daughter's life is at stake. I can't lose her like I lost Jamison.

I GLANCED UP. "WHO IS JAMISON?"

Heath shrugged. "From what I can tell, he was your brother."

"Are we talking half or whole brother?"

"That's something I don't know." Heath looked apologetic, and the reality of more family out there, or possibly dead, sent equal parts frustration and happiness running through me. How hard would it have been to tell me I had a brother? Even if he wasn't full-blooded, I'd always known about Nina. Had my mother been trying to keep her dirty secrets from coming to light?

I touched the screen of his phone so it wouldn't go to sleep, reading the words over in my mind again. "Why did she put daughter's like that? She has two." Had it just been a mistake from a hunted woman? Or was it intentional? Heath wouldn't have the answers for that.

Something occurred to me as I thought over the situation.

"Wait, how did your father die?" I asked.

"He went into Boston to meet with your mother the night she was killed."

FOURTEEN

"Your father died the same night as my mother?" It was like my brain wouldn't process it until I'd repeated his words.

He nodded, his expression a mask. "I only knew parts of the story, but from what I've pieced together, my father and your mother had been working on something for quite a while."

"They weren't together or anything, right?" I asked. It was totally off topic, but the idea my mom and his dad might have dated and now I had an intense attraction to the son was morbid.

"No," he said, acting like it was the weirdest question I'd ever asked him. "He was still mourning my mother's death from several months before." His voice cracked on the part about his mother, and his eyes conveyed his sadness.

What had the dynamic been between Heath and Heath, Sr.? From the way he spoke, he loved and missed his mother, but maybe his father was more demanding? Controlling even?

I shouldn't have been disappointed. The letter had to be a clue for something, but maybe I was hoping it would name my father so I could figure out the rest of my powers and abilities.

"Do you think whoever killed my mother also killed your father?"

Heath stared out at the street, seconds passing before he turned and acknowledged I was still there.

"No. My father was torn apart, his entrails out on the pavement for everyone to see. He was hardly recognizable, except for the ring he wore."

"Wait a second," I said, holding up a finger. "You get mad at me for wanting to avenge the murder of my mother, and yet you have just as much right to investigate it yourself."

"I suspect your mother's death goes back to the Shadowmoon Coven, while my father's murder would be someone from my own pack. As the leader, I have to be careful with whom I suspect. And don't think for a second I haven't carried on my own investigation."

Shame filled me. I'd thought I was better than him for publicly fighting to find my mother's killer. He didn't have that luxury as his every move was scrutinized and his progress had to be ten times slower than mine. No wonder he'd been so angry when I'd accused him of the murders. He was trying to find the killer within his own pack, without the resources or the ability to ask too many people about it.

"I understand that much."

"Go to your appointment. You're already late. We're not going to solve their murders today." He blew out a breath, like it was the thing he'd been holding out hope for.

He didn't give me another glance, only waited for me to leave the car.

I took the stairs instead of the elevator to get to Dr. Stringer's office, my brain going a hundred miles an hour with all I'd just learned.

My mind turned back to the letter. I needed to find clues, and I needed them fast.

The prickling sensation I'd gotten so many times before sent goosebumps along my arms and an urgency pressed against my chest.

It would be a lot easier if the sensation would whisper what the coming danger was. Something connected to my mother's murder? To Nina's blackouts? Or to the deaths of the shifters and Alina's case?

Once I was in Dr. Stringer's office, I still hadn't concluded what to make of all it.

I knew the whole of the bruja lands were subject to one coven, the Shadowmoon Coven. In some ways it should be easier than dealing with three vampire covens, but after the warnings I'd gotten from Tork and Heath, I knew it would be more difficult to find answers than I wanted, if I ever got into their territory.

"Claire, so good to see you today," Dr. Stringer said, walking into her office. "How are you doing?"

I shoved the new information into a box, locking it with an imaginary key. I already had enough issues to deal with and didn't want to be here until I was ready for retirement. Tork had met with Dr. Stringer frequently and because she was a paranormal helped me ease into the couch a little more, but I still didn't enjoy having someone in my head.

"I'm good. I had a strange headache yesterday." Even thinking about it caused a phantom pain to creep up, and I just hoped it wouldn't take hold.

She stared at me over her spectacles, pen in hand, poised to write. "What kind of headache?"

Just thinking about it sent my muscles clenching. "It was a piercing one, and I couldn't move for a few minutes. Then it continued to linger throughout the day, at least until the medicine kicked in."

"Where did this occur?" She definitely got straight to the point, something I appreciated.

"I was investigating a case near the Shadowmoon Coven lands."

She gave me a quick smile. "So Tork told you. I was wondering when you'd find out about my powers."

"You're the first paranormal not to wonder which box I fit into." At least I could be honest about most things when I came to her. I didn't have to pretend I wasn't some paranormal anymore.

"All in good time, Claire. We've got a lot of unpacking to do, anyway." She glanced back at her notebook and then back up at me. "How long were you there? In the bruja lands?"

I thought back to our conversation with Mary, trying to gauge the time it took for the interview and searching for the crime scene.

"We went to talk to the mother of a victim, and then she pointed us to where the body had been found. I went with my partner to the spot hoping to find some t—" and I paused, trying to think of a way to cover this up. I hadn't talked to her about the *tvary* yet, and the less people who knew about my gift, the better. "Traces of evidence."

"It would be hard to find them if this is a cold case, right?" Dr. Stringer asked, readjusting her glasses.

I nodded, glancing down at my hands. "It's always worth a look to see if anything was missed."

"May I ask the case you're looking into?"

"The murder of Alina Young."

Dr. Stringer sucked in a breath. "That was a rough one for the paranormal community."

"Wait, you heard about it? I thought the bruja coven was like a prison and nothing got out."

She shook her head. "It's hard to keep something like burns

from spreading. Then again, I'm an elemental and we can feel energy like that being sucked from a person. One of my sisters said the magic used was very powerful."

"Is there a diviner, like Evelyn, who could help us figure out who the killer was?"

With a smile, Dr. Stringer said, "Going back several years would drain her of her powers without getting you an answer. But if you have something more recent, she could take a look."

"There is the body of a teenage boy, a bird shifter at the morgue. We'd appreciate any help you could give us on this."

"When did your headache subside?" Her nervous tone caused my stomach to tighten. It was like she hadn't even cared about the young man who'd died.

I frowned, confused why she kept circling back to the headache. "I went back to the precinct and took some medicine. I didn't notice it after about an hour. Is there something wrong?"

"And did you have any lingering effects today?" She lifted her hand from the pad of paper and glanced up at me.

I shook my head, wondering what kind of lingering effects I could have after searching for a body.

She leaned over her notebook and stared at me. "Please call me the minute you have something like this happen again."

I stared at her in horror. The pain alone was excruciating, and I didn't want to endure it again, especially not when I needed to be focused for my job. "You think it'll happen again?"

"I'm almost sure of it."

FIFTEEN

"You're joking, right? What causes it then?" If there was a way to avoid the stabbing pain, I would take precautions to do it.

Dr. Stringer's phone rang. She glanced down at the number, her face draining of color. "I need to take this."

We both rose from our seats, and she ushered me to the door. "Make sure to schedule your next appointment with the receptionist and it was good to see you, Claire." She shut the door behind me and I paused at the door, curious about what could've been so urgent to cut our meeting short.

All I could hear through the door were mumbles and I walked toward the lobby.

Why did it seem like every time I thought I was getting closer to answers, I ended up taking two steps back in confusion?

For all Dr. Stringer's questions and concern over the headaches, I guess she didn't consider them emergency level stuff.

It wasn't fair she just dropped a bomb like that and then left. I'd never had something rock me to my core quite like the pain from these headaches. And the idea it would happen again scared me. I could handle pain, but this had been something different, like it was drilling into my mind.

Once outside her office, I realized my ride was no longer there. Tork was going to grill me about being late to work, when I finally made it. But maybe a walk to the precinct would help me get things into perspective.

I turned and started toward the precinct, I hoped, when I got a call from Nina.

"What time will you be home tonight?"

"Not until late. I'll just grab something for dinner," I said. I needed to head over to the cottage to look for some information about what was going on. Maybe Olivia Beckett/Belinda Sanchez had left some more clues for her daughters so we could figure out who we were and what talents we might possess.

I was still irked by the fact she'd mentioned only one daughter in her letter. It had to be a misspelling. She loved both of us like we were her only treasures on earth.

"What are your plans?"

It was still strange checking in with someone. I mean, I used to check in with Tori all the time, but I'd avoided doing so with Nina as much as possible when we'd lived together before.

"Job searching. Not the most exciting night, but I need to do something. Walking around this city and sitting in your apartment are driving me crazy."

"Any more dreams?" I asked, my voice sounding breathy. I needed to get back to a regular running routine. But so much of my time was spent combing through the cottage now that it was dark when I could get out. And after my adventures with the vampires, I figured I'd wait to test their abilities until I had some more of my own I was confident in using.

Another call came through and I saw Tork's name, silencing it as I waited for Nina to answer.

"No, and there's no feeling of motivation for anything. I might head back to Boston for a few days and stay with a friend. Then maybe I'll figure out why I needed to be back on the East Coast."

"That could work. Maybe head out there Saturday afternoon? The Mayor is bugging me to go through the things in his shed. I figured you'd want to keep some of the stuff?"

"Yeah, I can do that. I'll plan to stay with my friend for the rest of the weekend."

The buzz of another call came through and I saw it was Tork again.

"Sorry, I've got a work call. I'll talk to you later."

"No worries. Good luck."

I ended the call with Nina and answered the other call.

"What's up?" I said, trying to keep my frustration to myself. I'd been hoping to get some more answers from my sister, and Tork had never been this persistent before.

"You're going to want to get over here."

"Why, what happened? More bodies?" My mind spun with the possibilities of an urgent call from Tork to me. I had to be involved somehow, or he would've just asked Gonzalez or Newton to take care of the issue.

"You've got an invitation of sorts." I tried to picture what kind of invitation I would've gotten here in the city. I was so new that the only events I'd been invited to were security posts as a police officer.

I picked up my pace and said, "Invitation to what?"

His voice sounded almost giddy as he said, "You're just going to have to see it."

I hung up the phone, tucking it into the pocket of my jacket and jogged. I was only a few blocks away at this point and with every stride, I was amazed by the lack of pain from both my ankle and the gunshot wound in my thigh. Whatever gene allowed me that kind of relief was amazing. If only it could ward off splitting headaches.

A car pulled up alongside me and honked. I turned, ready to flip the driver off when I saw Heath's wide grin.

"Do you still need a ride? Or do you want to finish off your run there?"

Heat flamed my cheeks, and I closed my eyes, not trying to picture Heath watching me run from the backside.

I slid into the passenger seat and said, "Shut up and drive. Tork said it's important."

"You didn't want to try the bus system, huh?" Heath said, unable to stop grinning. Why was the guy so damn hot? I had to look out the windshield to have any hopes for my body to settle down.

"I'm an expert at public transportation in Boston," I said, tilting my head a little so my expression was a bit more challenging. "But here, I haven't even seen a bus stop."

"Yeah, the transit system here isn't up to par with Boston. It would probably take you a day to get to the precinct from here." He drove forward, one hand up on the steering wheel and the other resting on top of the automatic shift handle. "I got my mechanic to look at your car. He says it's ready for the junkyard."

I gasped, resting my hand over my heart to make it more dramatic.

"How could you say that about Sonja?"

He gave me a dry look and shrugged. "Someone's got to tell you the truth. That vehicle was ready for retirement at least ten years ago."

Tilting my chin up a bit, I said, "The benefit of living in Boston is you don't have to use your vehicle often, so pretty much I just saved ten years by parking it in the garage." It wasn't logical, but I didn't care.

Heath drove through the streets like the pro he was, and I had to admit I really liked his car. It wasn't obvious I liked sporty cars like this based on the scrap heap I called mine, but I'd always been a fan of the looks of them. They just made me smile.

A memory popped up. A man with a face I couldn't make out was holding my hand and walking around a lot full of cars, all makes and models. There had been a section of older cars and one of sports cars. From the perspective of the memory, I had to be young. Was he my father?

"You look like you're enjoying yourself," Heath said. His eyes glowed an amber color, and I wondered why it was. They were usually a dark chocolate brown with amber flecks.

"You're not a werewolf, right?" He rolled his eyes, looking at me out of the corner of his eye. His lips pursed like he couldn't believe I'd just asked that.

"No. I have control of my wolf form and my human form."

I thought about vampires, how their red irises meant they were hungry.

"What happens when your irises are amber colored?" I'd never seen a grin fall from his face so fast. "Is it because you're hungry, like the vampires?"

He glanced away and said gruffly, "I'm always hungry so it explains nothing."

I got the feeling he was trying to cover up something, his expression unreadable. I'd just have to ask Tork. He could be my non-attractive book of knowledge about the wolf shifters.

We got to the precinct, and I hurried in, trying to figure out what kind of invitation I'd gotten and why. Heath knew nothing about it, and the chances of me being invited over to the Dark Raider or Onyx Mark vampire covens for dinner were slim to none.

"What was such a big deal?" I asked. Tork turned around and smiled. He gestured to my desk where an envelope sat. I stepped over and picked it up. It was much heavier than a normal envelope, and the calligraphy of my name printed on front was unlike anything I'd ever seen. I turned it over, seeing the red wax seal of a bird. Who used these anymore? Wasn't it just easier to email or text?

"Who brought this by?" I asked. I slid my finger through the flap, but it didn't give like a normal envelope. Heath walked up behind me, the smell of his cologne causing me to turn.

"Of course you would think you could just rip it open like a regular envelope." He pulled out a small pocketknife with an insignia that matched the tattoo behind his ear, the arrows and the letters HL on the side of the case. Pocket knives seemed more like a Boy Scout type of thing to carry around. He was definitely Mr. Prepared.

I took the knife from him, shrugging off the zip of excitement from touching his fingers. Was I turning into one of those Regency women who got excited about something as small as that?

Shaking off the thought, I made a quick slash through the parchment, extracting the papers inside.

DETECTIVE CLAIRE BECKETT,

WE RECEIVED *word you visited the bruja lands without requesting authorization from the Shadowmoon Coven Council first. You are hereby summoned to come before The Council Saturday at eight in the evening.*

Be punctual and bring no one else with you.

WITH POWER,
The Grand Mistress

"WOW," I said, shaking my head. "Is this really how the bruja coven is?"

"What do you mean?" Tork asked, using a toothpick between his front teeth.

"Are they always this demanding? And do they have the authority to command me there? I thought the shifters were the leaders of Crescent City."

Tork shifted. "The shifters are in control, but we tread lightly when it comes to the witches."

Heath grabbed the note from my hand, his eyes roaming over the words. "We just came to an agreement with the bruja last week about working with the Crescent City PPD. Why would they do this? I'll have to call up the liaison and give them shit. We're supposed to have access to help them with any crime, as well as investigate other crimes if we have evidence to search." As he ran a hand through his hair, I had to hold back a smile. The man was even more sexy when he was irritated.

"Who cares how they are?" Tork said, chuckling a bit. "At least we have an in. It's more than I had when I started this division. Let's wait to rat them out and see how this plays."

I might have blinked a few times at the bluntness of Tork's request. Over the time since I'd been in the city, I'd only ever see Tork submit to the commands of Heath, not challenge them.

And in a surprising turn of events, Heath nodded, the determination in his jaw easing up a bit. "Yeah, it might be a good call. It will be a test of how they abide by the law they signed."

"Why can't they just meet with me now? Why wait until tomorrow night?" I asked.

"Do you think you're ready to face them now?" Heath asked, narrowing his eyes at me. There was a hint of amber there for a few seconds before they went back to their dark chocolate brown. Once he left, I needed to have a conversation with Tork to get it figured out.

"Of course I'm ready," I said, facing Heath. "I've survived the shapeshifter attack and a pack of vampires—"

"Coven of vampires," he said, looking amused by my statement.

Shaking my head, I said, "Whatever. I'm just ready for another girl to receive justice and maybe get a few questions of my own answered in the process."

The question was whether they would give me the answers I sought.

"Listen to him," Tork said, motioning toward Heath. "He knows what he's talking about, especially after negotiating with them for the past several years. Some extra practice to hone a few skills and walk through possible situations would be ideal, especially since your lightning isn't the most reliable."

I scowled at him, my ego not liking his response. "What skills though?"

"We can work on a few on Saturday when you come empty my shed." Heath raised his eyebrows, as if waiting for my challenge.

"We're trying to find a murderer, *Mayor*," I said, adding emphasis to his name. "Your storage shed can wait."

Newton walked into the room. "Do we have any information from the coroner?" His northeastern accent mixed with the gravelly sound of his voice made me smile. Such a strange combination.

"Not yet," Tork said, glancing down at some paperwork on his desk. "She's working on the autopsy of the bird from the Shifter Games right now. We should know more in a few hours."

"Okay, so what's our plan? We've got about twenty-four hours before I have to be on bruja lands. I'd prefer to come back out alive." The thought of ending up like one of the victims made my stomach turn.

Tork pulled off his glasses and glanced at each of us in the room. "The best idea right now is for Beckett to work with Heath. Come up with a game plan, practice a few things you can do in case you're attacked by the bruja. The rest of us will keep working on the details of this case and try to get you any information you can use while in there."

Not the task I expected to be assigned, but it would work. I needed the confidence going into the spider's nest that, if need be, I could get myself back out.

"Where are we going to practice?" I asked, strolling out to the garage. The question sounded more intimate than it should've, but I kept my eyes forward, doing my best to stay professional.

"We'll head to my house. And the mechanic should be done, so I'll have him bring your car by."

I turned and gave him a small smile. "Thank you, for doing all that."

Heath blinked lazily and shrugged. "We can't have one of our detectives stranded every time she needs to be somewhere."

"Oh, so you take care of all the detectives, huh?" I opened the passenger door and watched as he walked around to the driver's side.

He shook his head. "Just the ones I'm sworn to protect."

ALL THE GOOD vibes I'd had about Heath when we got into his car had now disappeared. Frustration filled me, and I wanted to hit something just for a release. Boxing gloves sat over in the corner, and they would be more helpful than diving into my feelings and trying to figure out my magic.

"You need to anticipate their moves, Beckett," Heath said, circling me in the large gym at the south end of his mansion. "Learn to call on your magic."

I closed my eyes again, searching for any wisp of magic within me. Seconds ticked past and I tried to block the irritation as Heath's footsteps clicked around me.

"Will you stop walking?" I said, opening my eyes to glare at him. We'd been in this room for at least two hours and my patience had officially snapped.

"Did you feel anything?" he asked, his hands in his pants pockets. With his tie loosened and his jacket slung over a chair near the door, he looked casual. I just wished the attraction would cease and my heart would settle down.

I would be standing before the Shadowmoon Coven Council in a matter of hours. Even if I didn't care about my punishment for stepping onto their lands without permission, I wondered what they would do to me if they found out I was the daughter of Belinda Sanchez.

Staring at the floor, I said, "I felt nothing."

I heard the low, guttural growl and glanced back up at him. His dark brown eyes seemed nearly black, and I took a step back, going through scenarios of what I'd do if he were to attack.

Instead of jumping toward me, he strolled over to a small desk tucked into a corner. Flipping through the pages of a book on top of it, he used his finger to scan the page.

"What were the exact emotions you felt before you shot out the bolt of lightning?"

I mulled it over in my head. The exact emotions? I'd gone through at least a dozen in those moments before, but the one thought I'd had was I was probably going to die.

"Panic, fear. Those pretty much sum it up."

Heath frowned. "Those are unstable emotions. We need to make you in control of your powers, not rely on them only at the last second."

"So how do I channel it from a place not born of fear?"

Seconds ticked by and Heath finally glanced up at me. Shaking his head, he said, "I don't know. This isn't something I've had to deal with before, being a shifter and all."

The sound of the clock chiming nine o'clock hit me. We'd gone over a few ideas, strategy-wise, but was there a way to block spells even if my magic wasn't working right now?

Where could I get answers?

The cottage.

"I'm going to head home. I'll head up to the cottage in the morning and see if there's anything I can find, any spells or tricks my mom left me."

Heath nodded, his jaw tight. "Let me know how I can help." The words had a dejected tone to them, like he hadn't been able to come in and save the day. I didn't really think of him as a white knight, since I'd gotten out of the crazy situations I'd been in the past few times, but it was nice to know I had people on my side.

"Will do," I said, grabbing my leather jacket from next to the door. I waved around the room and said, "Thanks for all this."

Heath snorted and gave me a half-smile. "For what? Lack of knowing how to summon your magic?"

Folding my jacket over my forearm, I turned to him. "Have you ever helped a bruja with her magic?"

"Once or twice." I waited for him to say more and when he didn't, decided not to press.

"I'm out. Thanks again for the car."

Instead of saying anything, Heath glanced back down at the books, turning a page here and there.

I stepped out of the gym and walked toward the front doors. My car was parked outside, and from the looks of it, someone had given it a good car wash and waxing. I turned back to look at the mansion, thinking of Heath.

Was this really just part of his job as a protector? Or was there something else going on?

SIXTEEN

I didn't sleep much that night, the anxiety of meeting up with a faceless council overrunning my dreams. Several times I lurched awake, my chest heaving and sweat trickling down my back. What would the bruja do if they ever found out who my mother was?

Probably kill me and use my body parts for one of their crazy spells, similar to ones I'd seen in books my mother kept.

At dawn, I headed to the cottage. It took some serious effort, but I got dressed and out of the house without waking up Nina. Grabbing a coffee and a bagel from the coffee shop, I steered Sonja to the grocery store for some lunch items and then toward the cottage. I wasn't sure what magic the mechanic had, but the ride was smooth and the engine started with no problem.

With a quick glance at the dashboard, I realized I had about fourteen hours until I had to stand before the bruja council.

I'd been able to find things in the cottage before, but would I find what I needed in time?

The phone rang, and Nina's name popped up as the caller.

"Where did you go?" she asked.

"Working on a case," I said. "I might be back in the after-noon, but I'm not sure." My brain glossed over the underlying panic simmering in my middle. I'd been nervous in a group of vampires a few weeks ago. For some reason, this was more than that.

"Okay, are we not meeting up to go through Mom's things?" Nina asked.

I groaned. "Do you mind if we do it another day? This case has me crazy trying to find a lead. I'll make sure Heath knows we won't be there yet."

"Works for me. I have to prepare for a job interview on Monday."

"Did you apply for some jobs?" I asked, shocked. I didn't think she was planning a permanent stay here. California had been her life for so long, I couldn't imagine her not there anymore.

"I saw a posting today and figured I'd apply. I doubt I have a shot in the news industry in California anymore and wanted to try here, since it's what I know." She paused, and I could hear the nerves in her voice when she spoke again. "I haven't gotten it yet. But it's a telephone interview with one of the stations in Boston. If all goes well, I'll have another interview in person next week."

"That's awesome, Nina," I said. It was kind of comforting to know she'd be around still, but also that we wouldn't be room-mates forever. I'd never had to wait so long for the bathroom to open up in my life. Okay, since we lived together several years ago.

"Thanks. I'm feeling good about it, but it could change between now and the phone call."

"Go prep for it and have fun with your friends. We'll plan a time next week to go through the stuff, before you start your job." I turned the wheel, getting ready to enter the woods. I'd probably lose service soon, so I had to hurry and end the call.

"Yeah, I'm open and it's not a done deal yet. It might be good to at least get rid of some of her stuff."

I waited a few seconds and said, "Maybe we'll find the bejeweled staff from your dreams." It was more of a joke, but would definitely be a bonus to cleaning out all the junk. It would be even better if we could find the Codex. If only I had it now, I'd take it as a peace offering to my meeting tonight.

Nina's voice trembled as she whispered, "Is it weird I'm a little afraid of it?"

I let out a short laugh. "Not at all."

"I mean, who knows? It might not even be a real thing and it could just be my psyche playing tricks on me."

My car moved over several bumps and I had to turn sharply, avoiding a large rock. That was the last thing I needed; to get stuck out in the woods with a flat tire.

"I wouldn't be so sure. I've learned a lot about dreams and other somewhat magical things since I moved here." I closed my mouth, wondering if I'd said too much.

"Magical things," Nina said, laughing. She stopped abruptly and said, "Oh, I got another call. Wish me luck!"

"You'll do awesome, Nina," I said. It was the first time I was really rooting for her.

Now I just needed to find a few spells to keep me alive after tonight.

SEVENTEEN

The path to the cottage seemed bumpier this morning, but the sun was just rising, and the colors it shot across the horizon were beautiful behind the towering pine trees. It was strange to come so early in the morning, as I was usually leaving when it was dark.

I'd brought a radio this time, hoping it would help me focus more on the information I was looking at, rather than all the strange creaking sounds of the cottage. And having lunch would mean I could research uninterrupted for several hours before my summons.

Using my hand to draw the signs in the air, I released the protective spell over the cottage and watched as it appeared again. When I had time, I'd have to bring some supplies to repair the structure. It would be nice to not worry about parts of it falling in while I was here researching things.

I opened the door and walked in, setting my water bottle and sandwich bag on the edge of the table. The air was stuffy, and I opened the window an inch or two, despite the few inches of snow on the ground.

I had already gone through several of the books sitting on the table, but then again, I hadn't been looking for anything specific. It wasn't the first time I'd wished for some kind of database where all this information could be easily searched, like a spell that could highlight the places in the cottage where the answers would be on any subject I needed.

But there was also something fun about the old pages, the books with the worn cover, and the idea my mother had used them at one time.

The shelves with neatly stacked bottles and tonics were still untouched since I'd come here. I figured I'd need a lot more knowledge before using any of them. After a quick scan of the books, I didn't find anything specific to defending oneself against bruja. Maybe it was an inherent trait? Or something I was supposed to learn from my parents growing up?

For the umpteenth time I wondered what my life would've been like if my mom had just told us where we came from and the powers we hold. How would I have turned out?

But would I have ended up like Alina, dead on the street corner?

Another scan for defensive skills turned up empty. I only had so much time and at least a thousand books in this place, so narrowing it down as much as possible was a must.

My attention caught on the small line hidden behind several books. I pulled them out, resting them on the desk. The line ended up being four lines connected to make a square.

A small lock was in the lower bottom corner, but instead of one small line like most locks, it was more of a z shape. I wasn't sure what I could use to open it. Where would my mom have kept something like that?

There was a rack of keys on the wall just inside the door but after a quick inspection, none of them were the specific shape I needed. Back near the wall box, I squatted down, trying to find any little canisters that might contain the key. Each one was filled with powders and trinkets, just no keys.

I tried to think of any hide and seek games I'd played with my mom when I was younger. Where was she known to hide? She was usually hidden in plain sight, sometimes covered in a blanket so it took longer than usual to find her. Could she have cut a small box into one of the books? Like those old-time people who hid a gun in a thick book.

That would be a lot of work to hide something so small. I opened a few of the books I'd moved, thumbing through the pages just in case. As I did so, the locket I always wore slipped from my neck fell to the ground. Picking it up, I noticed the clasp had broken.

I'd only had it happen once back when I lived in Boston. The impact with the ground had opened the locket and as I picked it up, I studied the picture of my mom. Her smile was vibrant, the exact thing that captivated so many people while she was a news anchor.

She'd put a picture of me as a small girl on the other side. It was right after I'd found a pair of scissors and chopped off the front section of my hair. It always made her laugh, but I looked like more of a boy than anything.

The edge of the picture of me was pulled up a bit on one side and I used my fingernail to pull it out more, curious if something had gotten behind it or a piece had broken from the impact on the floor.

Lifting one section, instead of the smooth metal I'd expected to see, there was a mechanism of some sort. Why would someone go to the trouble of doing this to a small locket?

Then again, when I looked at it from the side, it was thicker than I'd seen on other lockets through the years. I'd thought nothing of it, as my mom had said it was a family heirloom. From which part of our family, I now wondered.

As I went to push the picture back, the paper it was printed on was much thicker than usual photo paper. Maybe she'd written something to me on the back. She'd done it with the hundreds of pictures now stored in Heath's shed, ages and short descriptions of where we were in the photos.

It took a little tug, but I got the paper out. The back of it was a picture of a man who looked very familiar, but from where? Had I seen him before? And why would my mother put a picture of him in my locket?

I turned the picture so the man was facing out and pushed it inside. My picture was no longer visible. Things clicked and turned in, most likely the mechanism doing whatever its purpose was. The sounds stopped and then, at the bottom of the metal on the locket, a small key popped out.

"What the hell?"

I took the key and pressed it into the lock of the small box in the wall. It fit. Something about the whole situation caused a chill to run through me. I turned around, wondering how the locket had fallen in the first place, causing everything to line up.

I heard footsteps outside the cottage and froze. Sloan had mentioned there were a few others who knew of this place, but I had met no one since she'd shown it to me.

A few strides down the hall, and I was outside. "Hello?"

My gaze traveled along the tree line, looking for anything moving or some color that stood out. Nothing.

I breathed as shallowly as possible, half-expecting to hear footsteps or at least someone else breathing. Instead, there was complete silence.

"Okay," I said out loud, trying to calm myself. "This isn't bad, this is good. You're just a little freaked out by all the things you've learned over the past twelve weeks." And that I'd been carrying a secret key around my neck for the past twelve years.

All the revelations I'd received over time about my family, about my background, were adding up, and I had a feeling it wouldn't slow down. But each time something like this happened, it rocked my world, shaking everything I thought I'd known before.

Would the questions ever cease? Or would I be chasing clues of the woman I thought I knew as my mother had left behind for the rest of my life?

I turned the key in the lock, pausing a moment as I ran through the items she could've hidden in there.

Was it the Codex?

It could be jewels or money, but my mother had never been one for a gaudy amount of accessories and we'd been just fine on the money she earned from the news station, at least that's where I thought she got her money.

What if it was filled with cobwebs and spiders? I shuddered, not wanting to allow an infestation of the eight-legged insects to roam this now beloved cottage.

Taking in a deep breath, I pulled the door open. I'd never been so excited for a semi-empty compartment in my life. The box itself was at least two feet deep, making it look like a perfect cube from all the dimensions.

Inside sat one large box underneath what looked like several notebooks covered in cobwebs and dust. I pulled one out, swiping the dust away from the cover before opening the first page.

My mom's journals.

I flipped through, my heart breaking again as I recognized her handwriting, slightly different from the mature writing of her later years. Several lines carried both the snark and joking tone was Olivia Beckett, or as I now knew her, Belinda Sanchez.

The handwriting of this first journal was dated at least fifteen years before I was born.

"THINGS HAVE BEEN AWESOME LATELY, *and I can't believe all that's been happening. I found the best friends a bruja could ask for, and we've learned so much about using our magic over the past several months. Mother isn't happy, saying we'll be reported for using dark magic, but she thinks anything more than a cleaning spell is dark. She just likes to ruin all the fun.*"

IT TOOK a minute or two to do the math on the age my mother would have been.

Fifteen. Oh wow, she sounded way too much like me at that age. Although I was always grateful when my mom explained why she didn't want me to do certain things, the mention of my grandmother piqued my interest. My mom had spoken little about her in the years we lived together, and I wondered if the older woman was still alive.

I opened another journal, thinking I'd find a lot of the same. But it looked like these were dated four years later, when she was 19, and they had a much darker tone than the others.

"THE WHISPERS ARE ONLY GETTING LOUDER, *and I can't shake the feeling the ancestors aren't happy.*"

THE ANCESTORS? What was that all about?

I'd heard nothing about ancestors, but then again, I hadn't had time to grill Sloan about the beginnings of our species and all that.

. . .

"WITH SELENA GONE, *there's just the five of us. Our magic is weaker as a group, and I feel like I've lost the one person who could understand me in the world.*"

TEARS SPRANG to my eyes as I thought about Tori. We'd been through so much and I realized she'd come into my life about the same age as the previous journal entry I'd read.

What would it have been like to know someone your entire life and then lose them as a teenager?

I lost my mother at seventeen, and it was near devastating for me and Nina. As I thought about Alina's case, there had been six of them until only Alina was killed. I needed to talk to the rest of the group, even if it was just through handwriting and hand signals. Were they stashed somewhere in the coven lands?

The next entry was surprising.

"MY MOTHER TOLD *me I was getting a protector. It's the last thing I need right now, some shifter following me around, making me feel like I'm helpless. Why isn't there a bruja protection type of security? I'd be willing to train for that.*"

IT WAS the end of the entry and I wondered what would make the bruja coven so scared to have to enlist the shifters as their guardians and protectors. Heath would have more answers on that.

I scanned the next few entries, looking for anything important, but most of it was the musings of a nineteen-year-old girl.

She talked about a warlock she'd gone to school with and how they'd been hanging out more often.

For some reason, ever since I found out I came from witch stock, I had assumed their lives were completely different from mine. But as I read through my mother's words, it seemed she'd experienced all the highs and lows in life, only with a bit of magic mixed in.

Several pages were completely covered in black ink and I flipped through, coming to the end of that journal and picking up the next. I should be looking for defense spells or techniques I could use when meeting with the Shadowmoon Coven Council, but these journals held things I'd been looking for ever since she was murdered, and even more now since I lived in Crescent City.

A packet of papers fell out of the next journal, dropping to the floor. I bent down to pick them up and saw they were legal documents all stapled together. At the top it said Ray versus Clark. A quick scan told me this was a murder trial for the death of David Ray, whoever he was.

I'd been in the courtroom many times growing up, usually when my mom couldn't find a babysitter and had to go for her job. But this case didn't stick out as one I would know of. I placed the packet of papers on the table and glanced down at the several folded sheets on the inside of the notebook.

Opening the first, I saw Claire Sanchez-Clark. On top, it stated it was the birth certificate of the state of Massachusetts.

I glanced down and saw this birth certificate was not the same one I'd been using all my life. Instead of Olivia Beckett under my mom's name, Belinda Sanchez was printed. And with a quick glance over the name of the father, it took several moments for me to realize I'd been right. His name had been Henry Clark.

I glanced back at the court documents, scanning to see

Henry Clark was the name of the defendant on the case. Was my father a killer?

Moving my paper to the back of the other pages, the next birth certificate was for a boy born seven years before I was. Henry and Belinda were the listed parents once again. All the air rushed out of me, as if someone had punched me in the gut.

A brother. A full-blooded brother.

Jamison Sanchez-Clark.

I'd had a brother, and I could only hope I'd be able to find more information on him and my father, now that I had full names.

My moments of being happy about finding my mother's journals, now filled me with frustration. The only thing I'd ever wanted was an actual family; mother, father, and siblings who didn't completely hate me. At least this new reconciliation with Nina had helped fill some of that hole.

How hard would it have been to explain all this to me? I considered myself a valuable secret keeper, and could have done so as a teen.

Once again, I moved the certificate to the back of the stack and saw Karen Nina Danton. My heart floated in my chest as I glanced down at the mother line. Belinda Sanchez was not listed, but an Evelyn George Danton was. The father slot, which I was a little nervous about, wondering if she was my half-sister through my father instead of my mother, didn't list Henry Clark as the father.

This couldn't be right.

Nina wasn't my actual sister.

EIGHTEEN

It was official. My entire life had been a lie.

I had a brother or lost a brother I knew nothing about, and now my half-sister was actually the daughter of other people. Was that why Nina started having all the dreams?

What was I going to tell her? And was she even a paranormal?

My mind called up the picture on Heath's phone of the letter. No wonder my mother had only mentioned one daughter. But why would she have raised Nina as if she was her own?

My stomach clenched, and inside the anger and frustration only surged at the thought I was going to have to reveal this biggest secret of all to Nina. What would happen then?

"Hey sis, we're not really related. And I'm some type of bruja, but I'm not sure who you are yet."

That would go over well.

As much as I wanted to talk to her about it to find out what she knew and maybe piece some things together, it might be best to research our pedigree more. But at least I'd be there, ready to help guide her through the process of entering the paranormal world. Anything would be better than the non-answers I'd been given when I first got here.

I could be the person to help her, I just needed more time. We'd gone this long without knowing all the answers. A few more days wouldn't hurt.

My phone rang, and I knew it was Heath before even looking down.

"Where are you?" he asked, his voice sounding tired and frustrated.

"I'm in the woods," I said, deciding to avoid irritating him further. To be honest, I was more shocked at finding out the truth of my genealogy to give him shit.

"What's wrong?" he asked. It seemed to be his catch phrase every time he spoke with me these days. There were a lot of things that weren't right about what I'd just discovered.

It took a few seconds for my brain to come up with an answer. "I'm not sure. I just found something that could severely affect my relationship with Nina." Would she even want to be around me when she found out we weren't blood relatives?

I'd been alone for so long and the past week had been nice, having someone to check in with. Would I be okay if she stopped talking to me? Panic set in and I was tempted to tear up the birth certificate. No evidence would mean she wouldn't find out, right?

But the cop inside me knew I couldn't destroy something this important. No matter how much it would hurt, I'd survived two huge blows with the deaths of my mother and Tori. With time, I'd get over whatever happened.

"What could do that?" Heath asked, his voice rushed. A quick thought came to me and I wondered if he was more worried about what I'd found and if it connected to him. "I thought you were on good terms with her. Don't tell me you were a pain in the ass, as usual."

My face tightened, and I imagined it looked like the Wicked Witch of the West. "Well, for starters, I'm not a pain in the ass. We've been getting along really well, better than the past fifteen years in fact. But I found a birth certificate for an older brother I've never heard of. Secondly, my half-sister isn't even related to me."

"It's not the end of the world, Beckett. Nina will probably take it like you. Shocked at first and then determined to figure out the rest."

Something about those words said through his voice turned my frown into a smile. Every once in a while, I got a glimpse of how Heath saw me. But was I reading too much into this time? Probably.

"Did you find your own birth certificate?"

"Yes." I moved it to the top of the stack again. "It says my actual name is Claire Sanchez-Clark, daughter of Belinda Sanchez and Henry Clark."

"Oh, shit."

"What? What does it mean?" I hoped it was something good.

"It means we know exactly who and what you are."

A mix of relief and excitement zipped through me, and I waited for him to say something. I was finally going to have the full picture of my abilities and who I was, as a person and as a paranormal.

When he didn't respond, I said, "Dammit! Are you going to tell me or keep me in suspense all night?"

"We were right about the shifter part," he said, his voice lower than before. "But you're not a full fifty percent shifter."

What else could I be? Vampires were usually created by

other vampires and I'm pretty sure a ghost can't knock anyone up. Didn't shifters stick to their own group?

"Come on, Heath," I said, biting one nail as I stared at the stack of books next to me. My ass was sitting on the edge of the stool as I waited for his response.

"You're part elemental."

NINETEEN

"Me? An elemental?" I gave a half-laugh, not sure what it really meant.

I thought of Evelyn, the sketch artist who'd helped me track down Adam from the Unaligned Coven. Visions hadn't come to me, so I doubted I was a diviner. Dr. Stringer hadn't shown me any abilities in particular.

Did I just need another life-threatening situation to cause those skills to surface? If something like that caused them to surface.

"Are you sure he was part elemental?" I asked.

"I've never been more sure about anything in my life." His voice still sounded like he was in shock, and I wished we were on a video call so I could see his face.

I leaned over the table, resting my forehead in my hand as I tried to come to grips with this new revelation. After this, it would be nice to have an entire year with no surprises.

"An elemental? How is it even possible?"

Okay, I get how it's possible. My mother made sure I knew all about sex by the time I was entering junior high, but it would have been nice if she'd given me an example. Like, "Hey Claire, you're fifty percent bruja, and then twenty-five percent shifter and elemental."

I probably would have laughed.

"When a man and a woman love each other very much," Heath began, his sarcasm soaking the words.

"Really? What are you? Twelve?" I hoped Heath would tell me he was kidding or something. Being a bruja and a shifter was one thing. But adding a third paranormal in there was bound to make things a bit haywire.

"Oh, as long as your father is Henry Clark, I'm sure," he said. "He was one of the protectors who founded the Shifter Guard Organization. Actually, it was his father and when Henry was old enough, he helped continue it on."

"Okay, so did you know him? What can you tell me about him?" I needed details like I needed coffee in the morning, and right now, Heath wasn't giving them to me fast enough.

As I started thinking about the possibilities, I hoped I'd be able to at least meet some of my family. Then again, it seemed like they were all trying to stay away from me. But if my mom had kept this all from me, she probably kept it from everyone else, right?

"He was the ultimate shifter. One of the best at everything and would have been head alpha, except he declined to take part in the Shifter Games, saying he had enough on his plate as the head of the Guard. He wanted my father to be the head alpha."

Would I shift? Or did I have to be full-blooded to do that? What color would I be if I could shift?

The thoughts shot through my mind like lightning bolts, and I still couldn't believe we'd finally figured out my ancestry. And that Heath knew him made it even better. I had so many

questions and little time to get them in before my court appearance for the Shadowmoon Coven.

I'd pictured myself as a wolf ever since the injury to my
ankle and the speedy healing. Finally getting up the guts to ask,
I said, "What kind of shifter was he?"

I may have bitten my nail again as the suspense built. This
had to be the longest phone conversation we'd ever had.

"He was a salamander," Heath said.

What the hell?

That wasn't what I'd been expecting. Not a large, brooding
wolf? Or even a sly fox?

"Oh great, so I'm basically a reptile?" The thought of it was
so ridiculous I laughed. Instead of being a big, powerful animal,
I would be just as weak as always. And didn't salamanders have
sticky stuff all over them? I cringed just thinking about it.

"You don't understand. Salamanders control fire, and you
don't just shrink down into a tiny reptile. Henry turned into a
life-size salamander. It was intimidating, even scarier than my
father, to be honest."

I was still not convinced this was a good gift to have. "Okay,
so then what's the other half or fourth of me? What kind of
elemental was Henry?"

Heath let out a low chuckle and said, "I should've known
this the minute you displayed your electricity. Your grandmother was a lightning elemental."

'Was' seemed to be the keyword with everything in my life.
The chance to meet my grandma sounded like it had passed.

"So, what happened to him? Did he die?"

There was a long pause on the other end, and I prepared myself
for the truth: that everyone in my immediate family had died.

"No one knows. There were documents assigning the next
head of the Shifter Guard and directions for any other aspect of

his life. The Guard has searched for him over the past twenty-five years, but it seems he just vanished."

I glanced back down at the court case documents. "What about a murder? Was he ever accused of murdering anyone?"

"I don't know all the details, Beckett. I promised I'd help you figure out who your family was and is, and I'll still keep it. But you need to head back here soon. I'll meet you at your apartment and drive you out to the bruja lands."

"I can drive myself," I said, pulling my phone away from my ear for a moment to check the time. Already four-thirty.

"Yes, I know, but I'd feel safer if I dropped you off. Hopefully, the meeting will only last a couple of hours."

I closed my eyes, shaking my head at that thought. A meeting with a bunch of bruja for a "couple of hours" sounded like torture and no matter what, they'd find out who I was. Keeping the fact I was the daughter of Belinda Sanchez a secret would probably be my only means of getting out of there alive.

A sliver of self-doubt pierced what I'd thought had been impenetrable armor, and I said, "Do you think I can do this?"

"Can you live with yourself if you don't?" Heath asked. He had a point.

If Alina's case had come up as just a cold case, it wouldn't have been a rush to solve today. But we'd already lost at least five shifters and we couldn't afford to lose anymore, not without finding who the actual killer was. The several cats Gonzalez and Newton had found were real felines, which sliced through me harder than I'd expected.

"No," I said, a surge of immediacy hitting me. "I'll head out now."

"Drive safely." More than just him being my protector, my crush on the Mayor had grown from the tenderness in his voice with those two words. We hung up, and I stared straight ahead for several moments, feeling the exhaustion creep in. What a roller coaster my emotions had been on throughout the day.

I now had some missing puzzle pieces to my background, and I needed to learn more about them. A bruja who could wield fire and lightning sounded pretty intense. Maybe being a salamander wasn't a total loss.

Energy would be the key to making it through the night, meaning I needed to pick up a soda on my way back to the apartment.

I tucked the journals back into the wall box, locking it with the key from my locket and heading out to Sonja. It was unnerving to think I wasn't any more prepared for my meeting with the Shadowmoon Coven than when I'd gotten to the cottage that morning, but knowing more about my background gave me more confidence.

I hoped it would be enough.

TWENTY

"Beckett," Tork said over the phone as I made it to the main road. "Come in before heading to the council meeting. We've got more information for you."

Instead of turning right, I turned left, making my way toward the precinct. I hoped this wouldn't take too long. A shower was necessary before I headed out for the night's meeting.

I thought about what I would say, how I could slyly get answers to my mother's role in the coven, and maybe a few clues about what the Codex looked like, but it might be a dead giveaway about my identity. A summons to a council such as this only meant I wouldn't have time for my own agenda.

"What have we found out about the Michaels' case?" I asked, striding into the precinct. It was the first time the four of us had been in the same room in a couple of weeks. All we needed was Heath and Captain Woods to make an appearance and the group would feel complete.

Gonzalez stepped forward with several papers in his hands. "It looks like the girls were involved in something secretive. We found video evidence from three years ago outside their school."

"Wait a second, no one looked at this before?" I took the photos from him, surprised they were surveillance photos. They weren't the clearest pictures ever taken, but at least I got an idea of what the girls looked like. I had an inkling I wouldn't get to talk to them, but if I could pick them out of the crowd, maybe I'd find more answers.

The girls kept looking around, as if they were starting a drug ring in the middle of the bruja complex. They looked to be talking about something, their heads all bent together with a sly glance around them every so often.

"We only just got the cooperation of the bruja coven with our department last week," Tork said. "And no paranormal division equals no extra digging."

The team pulled up all the videos, displaying them on Tork's computer, and we watched as several students exited the school. When Alina came out, I recognized her, her fine features and long brown hair giving her away. She met up with the other five girls at the corner of the building, where the photos had been taken.

"Okay, so this must've been before they stopped hanging out together," I said, trying to put the events we knew of into sequential order in my brain.

Gonzalez pointed to the date, "Yeah, it's about two weeks before her death."

I wished I could see a clear picture of each of her friends, in case I saw them at the Council meeting. Mary Michaels had said a few of their names, but it was difficult to remember all after a few days. I should have taken better notes while I was there.

"Okay, I'm going to need everything you have on those girls." I pointed at the screen. But with negotiations between the bruja coven being so recent, I doubted we'd have much. Even finding their names again would be huge for me.

"Getting a little bossy, aren't we?" Tork said, chuckling.

I lifted my hands out to the sides. "Do you want this to work or not?"

My insides were already twisting at the thought of going before a bunch of powerful bruja, and my patience was thin. We had only a few hours before I had to be there and I was cursing, wishing I had more time to study this out.

I took a deep breath, knowing I didn't need to alienate my team. "Sorry, I just want this to pay off. And I'd love to be alive when I leave that meeting tonight."

Tork nodded and turned to Newton and Gonzalez. "I want as many details as you can find on these girls, or anything connected to the case before six-thirty. Send it right to Beckett. We need to give her the chance to brush up on it before she has to be there. I doubt we'll get any kind of phone service in there and a wire won't pass through their security."

I gave him a small smile, grateful we had enough people in our division now to split the workload, and that we were working toward a common cause.

As much as I'd loved the 27th precinct, I realized I'd been missing this chemistry there.

As all the guys either texted or emailed me or brought me sticky notes with little bits of information, I wrote them down in my small notebook, hoping if I got the chance to speak with any of the girls, I'd at least have something to ask to get more of the story.

Around seven o'clock, Tork walked up to my desk, laying several pieces of paper in front of me. "Here is some information on the ladies and gentlemen on the Council. There isn't much time, but at least you'll know names and faces."

The sincerity in his voice blew me away. We'd had our

differences in the short months since I'd come to Crescent City, but it seemed like Tork was coming around. He at least understood me a lot more than before.

That they were all worried about me sent a shiver of comfort running through me. It was like we were some deranged form of family.

"You've got this, kid."

I nodded, hoping to convince him of my courage. Inside, I was a ball of nerves.

"Good luck studying all this," Tork said, striding back to his desk. "Heath will be here in about fifteen minutes to pick you up."

I nodded, curious why he hadn't called me himself. Maybe he thought it would distract me from studying about the famous Crescent City bruja council. So much for getting a shower and a change of clothes.

"There really isn't a wire I can wear in there?" I asked, trying to lighten the mood.

Tork shook his head. "If only it were that easy. What you need to do is stay awhile and infiltrate their ranks. Then come back and tell us all about it." He was joking again, but the idea was somewhat appealing. An insider spy who could report on the antics of the bruja.

"Well," I said, "Let's see how this first meeting goes."

My stomach growled. I stood and walked toward the break room. Newton had ordered pizza for all of us and I'd already had at least four, maybe five, pieces. I grabbed another slice and took a big bite. I wasn't hungry but hoped to distract my nerves a bit by making my stomach overly uncomfortable.

As I leaned up against the counter and took another bite, I raised the sheet up so I could read Tork's handwriting. He'd written everything in capital letters and it was surprisingly neat.

Eleanor Grange-Grand Mistress of the Shadowmoon
Coven Council

Sage Michaels - First Assistant

Troy Beckinsale - Second Assistant

Alice Everly - Council Secretary

I noticed there wasn't a picture of the Grand Mistress, but I
needed to check the relationship between the first assistant and
the victim. It didn't take long to walk out of the break room and
over to Tork's desk.

Pointing to the picture above the words Sage Michaels, I
asked, "Is this lady related to Alina?"

He put on his glasses and leaned over. "Michaels is a
common name in the bruja world. Let's look her up."

He tapped a few keys, pulling up Sage in the database.

Gonzalez walked past and asked, "What are you guys
looking for?"

"One woman on the council has the same last name as the
victim. It might help to know if she was a close relative to
Alina." At least that's what I hoped. I lifted the paper so
Gonzalez could see it.

"There's actually an easier way to look it up," he said. He
walked around Tork's desk and took over the computer, typing
into the Internet browser.

CrescentCityPFT.com

"What's PFT?" Tork and I asked at the same time.

"Paranormal family tree," Gonzalez said, cracking a smile.
He'd been so solemn today, it was a nice break to see him in
better spirits.

Tork gestured to the computer screen. "How did you know
about this?" He placed his hand over the mouse as Gonzalez
gave up the reins.

"My grandma was one of the founders, along with several
of the ladies from the different groups and packs. They

recruited the older generation from each of the species, trying to make it easier for people to keep track of their lineage." He looked more bored than anything, probably never thinking we'd be able to use it in a case.

"It sounds weird, like some old person's hobby," I said, "but it may help us in this situation, right?"

There were several search boxes at the top, allowing us to search one name or connect a few.

Tork entered Sage and Alina's names in the boxes and pressed enter. The wheel of death greeted us, and I hoped it would come up before I had to leave for the meeting.

"Sorry," Gonzalez said, staring at the screen. "They didn't invest too much into the website part, mostly because they don't know about technology."

I laughed, picturing little old ladies trying to put together a website on their own. Hell, it was even above my capabilities.

The wheel disappeared and results finally popped up. It looked like a tournament bracket of sorts, with Alina on the one end and then what looked like Sage in a far-reaching branch.

"So, they're distantly related?" I asked.

"It looks like she's Alina's great aunt," Tork said. He moved his finger to the section just below both names. As much as I tried to concentrate on the names and their positioning in the bracket, I couldn't make a solid decision about where the two of them connected.

"Why wouldn't she push to have her great niece's death solved?" Gonzalez asked.

Tork shrugged. "That's what I would've done if in a place of power. One more thing you can learn tonight, Beckett," he said, giving me a small smile.

"Heath is outside," Newton said, coming from the garage.

"You've got this, Beckett. Let us know as soon as you're out what happened." A flicker of anxiety passed across Tork's face and it was nice to know other people were rooting for me, even if on the outside of the bruja lands.

I'd done everything I could to research the people and the places. The probability of me remembering all the information was slim, but maybe it would help keep me from having to fight anyone.

I wasn't ready for a physical skills test.

TWENTY-ONE

"You're white as the moon," Heath said, pointing up to the orb in the sky out the front windshield.

I looked over at him, trying to hold down the pizza I'd eaten an hour before. I wasn't sure I'd make it through the front gate, let alone the meeting, but the closer we got, the more I kept seeing Lee Vance's face morph and change before me as it had in the warehouse.

"After all this is over, can you help me convince the guys to look for Lee Vance?" I asked. Just saying his name out loud sent a shiver of fear running through me. I wouldn't be able to get rid of that feeling until the man was behind bars. Or dead.

"Still worried about him, huh?" Heath glanced over at me, his face impassive. I'd expected him to make fun of me, but I appreciated that he hadn't. This whole emotional rollercoaster was hard enough to navigate. I didn't need other people making it even more difficult to get back to normal.

I didn't want to show him weakness, but he'd already seen me in some of my most vulnerable states. I needed to be strong for this.

"It would help on so many levels to know the guy haunting my dreams and my day visions is behind bars." I blew out a breath, feeling just a smidge stronger after having admitted it. Dr. Stringer would be proud I'd actually acknowledged I wasn't perfect.

"Will do." Heath pulled up alongside the street where we'd visited Alina's mother earlier.

"This is as far as I'm allowed to go. But remember, you have your phone, which I've added a special line to, allowing me to get through some of the security measures."

"When did you have that done?" I asked, pointing to my phone.

He gave me a sheepish grin. "I might have had one of my guys make a duplicate when you first got to Crescent City. It's how I know exactly where you are."

"Can you listen in on my conversations?" I asked, my blood pressure rising.

"Yes," he said, his eyes narrowed in on my face. "But I don't. I only installed it so I wouldn't have to stalk you to keep you safe. I knew when they transferred you here from Boston that being tied down by rules wasn't the best way to protect you."

I nodded, trying to decide how I felt about someone tracking me for the past few months without my knowledge. But it made sense how he was able to get to all the crime scenes within a few minutes.

"Just call me and I'll break every rule I'm supposed to abide by to get to you."

I might've stared at his face a bit too long, not knowing whether to still be frightened about what was to come or to ponder a deeper meaning behind those words. There was such a fierceness to his expression I didn't doubt he would ruin the relationship he'd built with the bruja to keep me safe. I just hoped it had to do with a few extra feelings he had for me outside of being my protector.

"Thanks, Heath," I said. There was no sarcasm this time. We were a lot closer than we'd been in the past, but I didn't have time to dwell on our relationship. The council would be waiting, and I hoped this didn't turn into a bloodbath.

To be honest, I didn't want to be shedding any blood at all, my own or one of the bruja. Who knew? She could be a distant relation.

I was almost out of the car when Heath grabbed my hand, the warmth of his fingers holding onto my palm causing a hot flash through my body.

"Remember who you are. You could take down the council with a few words if you wanted to." The corner of his mouth lifted, and I felt the truth of his words hit me in the chest.

Without saying a word, I slipped out of the car, almost feeling like I was heading to my death. That's how everyone had talked about this meeting for the past twenty-six hours, like surviving it would be a miracle.

I straightened my shoulders, knowing if I were going to convince the council I was the badass detective I hoped to present, I'd need to start right now by convincing myself.

Once again at the tall iron gates, I breathed out, glancing up at the darkness nearly covering the sky as if it knew what was coming.

The gate was locked and it wasn't until Heath had pulled away that I heard the lock start to lift and the squeak as the gate opened. At least I wouldn't have to slam my fist into it like Newton had. I didn't even see damage on it from his hit.

"Detective Beckett," a voice said from behind the gate. It took a few seconds for my eyes to find the man dressed in all black with only his lips visible in the moonlight. "Thank you for accepting our request."

I nodded, knowing that keeping my mouth shut right now might keep me alive longer. It hadn't been a request, it had been a necessity.

"Please follow me," he said, taking long strides down the trail leading between several pine trees.

"Where will the Council meeting take place?" I finally asked. My brain was trying to pick anything out of the ordinary, hoping, if need be, I could find my way back to allied lands in an emergency. With all the trees, though, it was making it difficult to see any way out as we wound back and forth through them.

There had to be some crazy space spell going on with Crescent City, because on a map, the bruja lands looked as though they were only as big as the North End in Boston. But much like the shifter region and the vampire lands, I suspected they were at least two times the size, if not bigger.

The man never answered my question, but I kept following, wishing I could've worn a wire or something to know I had my team at my back. But at least whatever Heath had done to my phone might work. I'd just hope it didn't run out of battery by the time I needed it.

The man stopped, and I almost ran into him. Doing a quick sidestep, we avoided a collision.

Putting his hand out and waving it a few times, he mumbled some words. The trees parted and a large building lit up like a Christmas tree stood before us. It was something. It made me feel like the small invisibility spell I cast over the cottage was nothing more than a child's magic trick.

He walked up and opened the door, never pulling back the hood of his cloak. Once inside, he made me take off my shoes, and gave me a black cloak of my own.

"Is this all really necessary?" I asked, my tone adding a bite to it. Being ordered to do anything out of my comfort zone wasn't something I usually participated in willingly. But taking off my boots meant not being fully prepared to run should I need to.

"That's the protocol for all visitors," the man said and waited for me to walk through to the next room.

Once inside, a searing pain hit my forehead and I had to breathe through it, slow painful breaths. It wasn't the kind of pain from a migraine, although some of the effects of it were. No spots in my vision, no throwing up, but it was like it hit my head first and then slowly drifted down into my chest, squeezing until the air made it hard to breathe.

"Are you all right?" a bruja asked me. I hadn't seen her there, and my insides jumped at her voice.

"I'll be fine," I said, rubbing my forehead with an intensity I'd never had to use before. Focus, I just had to focus. This was one of the biggest breakthroughs for the paranormal division, the chance to stand before the bruja council, and I needed to be sharp and ready to report back on anything I noticed while here.

The woman gestured down to where a light was shining on a large podium and I could see a few sections of benches lined up. It was nothing like the Shifter Games, but I also wasn't at ease the way I'd been there.

"You'll step up to the platform in the middle of the room," she said, holding up a small circle in front of my eyes. "This is used to amplify your voice, allowing the entire room to hear you. I'll be placing it right here against your Adam's apple."

I wasn't sure what was worse, the cold metal or her freezing fingers against my skin. There was a slight tingle where the metal sat, and I wondered how sensitive the sound was. Could they all hear my breathing? My heartbeat?

"I hope you understand this is a rare occurrence," the woman said. I could see the bright red of her lipstick and the slightly pointed nose peeking through the hood. "You will address the Council using the terms Mistress and Master. But the Grand Mistress is only addressed as such, so don't forget it."

She adjusted my cloak hood so it was back to my hairline, revealing my face. "What's the point of the cloak then?" I asked.

"We believe in a uniform society," the woman said, her tone foreboding.

She gave me a gentle push and after a quick stumble, from which I'd recovered, I walked up to the podium in the middle of what looked to be a circular theater. A quick glance around showed me dozens of bruja who'd turned out to see these proceedings. Were they all part of the Council?

The ache in my forehead subsided enough to breathe normally, and I hoped it would last throughout the duration of the meeting.

The six people I needed to worry about were sitting up in front, on the bottom row. They hadn't bothered to cover themselves, their hoods laying against the back of their cloaks.

"How was that unified?" I wanted to ask the woman again. At least I had some spirit left in me, even though every muscle in my body was clenched in a fight-or-flight response.

A chime filled the air, and the group rose, all turning toward something at my left. A figure walked in, taking a seat in the middle of the six people.

Once settled in, the woman threw her hood back and I gasped, trying to keep my discomfort from showing. The woman sitting in the position of Grand Mistress was Adelaide, the woman who'd been friends with my mother and who'd fled the grocery store the moment I spoke of magic. If I'd known she was here, I'd have done something to be summoned much earlier.

She had to have the answers I needed.

"Detective Beckett," Adelaide said. "I'm the Grand Mistress Eleanor Grange and this is the rest of the Shadowmoon Coven Council."

She pursed her lips, interlocking her fingers and staring at me. I looked for any recognition but nothing signaled she knew who I was past being a detective. "This is very unusual, but we have forsworn tradition and invited you here as you are seeking the murderer of Alina Young."

She stopped talking and I could've heard a pin drop with the amount of silence echoing through the air.

"Is it true?" one of the men asked when I didn't respond.

"Sorry, yes. The Crescent City PPD have been searching for the killer of several shifters and believe there to be a connection with the death of Alina Young. We hope that by finding the killer, we'll save lives both in the bruja and the shifter groups."

The chatter in the room increased after my statement, and I could hear some of them talking about how they didn't care what happened to the shifters. Statements like this burned me up. The life of every person and creature was worth it to me.

"And what conclusions have you come to so far?" the Grand Mistress asked.

How much did I divulge to these strangers? Were they going to help me? Or would I be looking over my shoulder at all times after I left the bruja lands tonight?

"My partner and I came to speak with Mrs. Michaels about the details surrounding her daughter's death. We spoke for some time, mostly about her daughter's friends," I said, letting my gaze dart around the room, trying to absorb every element and face I could. It was possible the killer was in this room.

"We've had reports you were searching around the scene of the crime," another woman on the council, this one matching the picture of the woman related to Alina, challenged me.

"Yes," I said, avoiding mention of *tvary*. I couldn't trust them with something so important. "It always helps to go over a crime scene, just to see if I can get a better picture of what happened." See what I did there?

"But three years later?" another man asked.

"It's a cold case," I said. "I have to start somewhere. The only information we had was she was killed and the spot where she was killed. The paranormal division is newer, but wouldn't it be a good thing if the Shadowmoon Coven worked together with the police? We want to find justice for the victim, but we can't do it without the proper information or any interviews that might provide more insight into what spurred the killing." I'd probably said too much, but I focused on relaxing my breathing after spitting out that many accusations.

The Grand Mistress stared at me for some time, her gaze so intense I was sure she could see into my soul. How could she not know it was me? Did she have some kind of amnesia after our encounter?

Instead of scrutinizing me like the daughter of a thief to this coven, she glanced down at the papers.

"We shall allow you to stay within the Shadowmoon Coven lands for the duration of the next two weeks. If you're able to uncover the murderer, we will negotiate better terms for the paranormal division."

"And if I don't solve it?" I raised an eyebrow, curious as to the lengths these people would go for punishment.

The Grand Mistress glared down at me, and I couldn't help but wonder if meeting her had just been a fluke, or if she was just pretending not to know who I was.

"Solve it." The woman's voice echoed around the room with all the force of tyranny.

It was a risky move, but I couldn't help but grin widely. "Will do. What time should I return tomorrow?"

"I don't think you heard the Grand Mistress correctly," Alina's great aunt said. "You will not leave our lands until you solve the case."

My grin faded as the truth of the situation dawned on me. How would I solve a case with no resources?

"Can I at least have another member of my team here?" I tried to make it sound direct and commanding, but it ended up shaky. I could see the answer already on the head woman's face.

"I deny your request," the Grand Mistress said, tapping something long and skinny against the table. It wasn't a wand, but as I looked closer, I gasped internally. It looked like a rod with a jewel in the hilt, just like Nina had described from her dreams.

Oh shit. I was in trouble.

"Sage Michaels will show you to your living quarters and you will begin investigating in the morning. Anything you need, it will give you based on the idea that you will ask before investigating it."

She must've known me, or at least read the person I was. Asking permission wasn't usually something I did. It was easier to ask forgiveness after the fact, but the consequences didn't always go my way. Like how I ended up transferred to a new precinct, which I didn't want to repeat.

"You want me to take her around, Grand Mistress?" Sage asked, looking less than thrilled with this assignment.

"I prefer someone I trust following her around. Make sure she stays out of trouble and the restricted areas." The two of them stared at each other for several awkward seconds, and I wondered if they were speaking through telepathy.

A scream in the back of the room caused everyone to turn. My eyes scanned the room, looking for any sign of distress. Behind me, a section of people looked down at something. My police instincts kicked in, and I turned, running up one aisle. Running in socks on concrete stairs was not easy.

"Detective Beckett," the Grand Mistress called to my back. "We are not done."

I stopped midway up the aisle, turning to glare at her. "If there's someone in distress, I'm obligated to help. So, if you need to shoot me with magic because I'm trying to help one of your own, what does that make you?" She kept staring but didn't act.

I turned and continued to run up the steps, half-braced for impact as I expected to be zapped for not listening to her. Once I made it to the top of the stands, I saw a body on the ground. She was young, maybe eighteen or nineteen. Her eyes were closed and as I checked for breathing and a pulse, I found none.

Glancing up at the people who'd been standing around her, I asked, "Did you see anything? What happened?"

The other two girls shook their heads and the one with a pixie cut said, "We were just listening to the proceedings when she screamed and fell backwards."

That didn't help me at all. I leaned over, trying to figure out what Stacia would do if she were here. Maybe CPR?

I didn't have many chances to come upon a body before the body temperature was already down. Twice I had, Tori and my mother, but it was already too late then.

"What are you doing, Detective Beckett?" I heard behind me. I glanced over my shoulder and saw Alina's great aunt scowl directed at me.

"I'm trying to save her," I said. What was with all these people? They all just stood staring at the body. Did they not have a sympathetic bone in their bodies?

I'd only done about five compressions when my hands heated, as if I'd stuck them directly into a fire. For a moment I panicked, thinking that of all the times my fire powers could manifest, right now was probably the worst.

But as I pulled my hands back, I saw the cause of the burning. Holes appeared in her chest and in her abdomen, the clothing melting into her skin and showing the blood inside. I had to take a few breaths before I looked closer, keeping the pizza lodged in my throat instead of all over the body.

It looked identical to Alina's murder scene photos, except this time, I was close enough to see the heart and what looked like the liver on one side was gone.

I couldn't remember if those were the same organs gone from Alina's body or not.

I turned around to the group and stood. "What could've caused this? Is there a spell or—?" I couldn't think of anything else, and hoped one of them would continue with my thought process.

What could burn a person from the inside out?

The room was silent and I knew there had to be someone with the knowledge to do this.

"Grand Mistress, lock down the building. No one is leaving until we have more answers."

TWENTY-TWO

Either the nearly one hundred bruja in the room had no idea what happened, or they were really good at lying. If I were an empath, I'd be able to tell if they were innocent, but it hadn't been one of the several skill sets I'd inherited, at least not what Heath had described.

Lightning, yes. Healing could count for the shifter part. But the rest was unknown. At least I was getting better at physical cues, thanks to Newton's guidance.

As I glanced around at the bruja closest to the body, there was genuine panic. This happened to Alina, and several shifters out in the city, but had it happened before?

I pulled out my phone, trying to find Stacia's number. If she could tell me at least what would have caused such holes, I might have a better way to narrow down my suspects so I wouldn't be stuck in this room all night.

My fingers moved too fast and I had to keep scrolling up and down, finally locating her number. I dialed it, crying out when someone grabbed my phone for me.

"You're not allowed to make phone calls here," the Grand Mistress said, nodding at Sage, who'd yanked my phone away.

Gritting my teeth, I said, "I'm a detective for the Crescent City Paranormal Police Department. This is part of my job and this woman is part of my district. Do you want this to keep happening to your people? Don't you see the fear in your coven because of this?" I motioned to the group around, several of them inching back as much as possible.

I saw the Grand Mistress' lips twitch and held back a smile, hoping I would win out in the end.

"You can make one phone call," she said, motioning for Sage to hand my phone back to me.

"What happens if she doesn't answer? She's the coroner for the entire city. It's not like she can just grab her phone at all times," I said. Sure, I wasn't the best with authority, but the fact this woman was trying to obstruct the ability to do my job didn't help.

I redialed Stacia's number, hoping she'd answer. Several rings sounded and ended up going to her voicemail. I ended the call and went back through my contacts, stopping on Tork's number.

With a quick glance back toward the Grand Mistress, I said, "I'm calling someone else at the precinct." My thumb hovered over his number and then I remembered I probably wouldn't get through to Tork even if I tried.

Heath had made it so I could get directly to him, meaning he was my best shot right now. Scrolling to his name, I glanced back up, waiting to see if the Grand Mistress would do anything.

It was like swallowing my pride, but every second we could figure out what was causing the holes might save the body enough stress to find out what caused this.

The woman turned up her nose but nodded, looking less

than enthused about me, the outsider, coming into her territory and making demands. The phone only rang once and his deep voice came on the line.

"Beckett? What's wrong? Are you done already?" Hearing him speak made me wish I'd never come in here. But then would more innocent bruja die? All because I was too scared to face my family ancestry and do my job? At least they hadn't figured out who I was yet. Or so I hoped.

"I need you to get in touch with Stacia," I said, turning back to the body. The wounds were even darker now, and I hoped we weren't too late to figure out what happened. Not that I wished anyone dead, but this bruja had died here while I was researching the death of Alina, would hopefully lead to some more clues.

"Stacia? Why do you need Stacia? What happened, Claire?" He was more worried than I thought. He rarely called me Claire.

"A bruja died during the meeting. She's got all the same markers we've found on the shifters," I said, aware I had at least twenty-five bruja in the vicinity staring me down and waiting for me to figure this out.

"I'm coming in," he said, and I heard the car door open.

"No! Don't come in. They've told me I'm the only one allowed in here." Now that I thought about it, this was more like a hostage situation than anything. I just had to remember those skills as I worked through this murder and Alina's. "Get Stacia on the phone. I need to figure out what is causing the burn holes."

"Did you call her?"

"Really, Heath? Really? I got one phone call, and she didn't answer, so I called you. Will you find her already?"

"Give me five minutes," he said. The line went dead, and I slid my phone into my jacket pocket. With all the witches standing around me, I shifted from one foot to the other, feeling more like I needed to give them a play-by-play so they wouldn't cast a hex on me or anything.

I'd read about a few of them in some of my mother's books, and they sounded nasty. Most didn't kill the person hexed, but I didn't want to take any chances. And I definitely didn't want to end up like the girl on the floor.

"He's going to call me right back." I pointed to my feet. "I'd like my boots back... please." I added the please after a few seconds delay, knowing happy bruja meant I kept breathing.

The Grand Mistress waved to the other bruja and said, "The rest of you go home now. We will reconvene as soon as we have any news about the death of Flora."

"We can't clear the crime scene until I have statements from everyone," I ground out. "Anyone could be a suspect here."

With an icy glare, the Grand Mistress said, "This is the Shadowmoon Coven. No one may enter or exit the premises without permission from the council, punishable by death." She'd punctuated the last three words, sending a clear signal she was the boss. "So, if you need a conversation with each of them, you will do so outside the building of a crime scene."

I swiped my tongue along my lips, feeling suddenly dehydrated. The pressure of the headache returned, causing me to crouch down next to the body.

Footsteps sounded along the floor as the bruja filed away, leaving me, the Grand Mistress, Sage, and two of the Council. Another one returned with my boots.

Minutes ticked by and the headache eased up, allowing me to breathe normally and focus on the task at hand. At least it hadn't lasted minutes like the last one had.

The silence was awkward and tangible, but I focused on the body, hoping to find something, maybe even some *tvary*.

The bruja, whom I guessed was named Flora, was dressed in what looked to be rather plain clothes, a long, A-line skirt in black and a purple blouse. I guess they stuck true to the way stories portrayed them. There were no warts or broken pointy noses, so it must have been the spin humans put on them.

As I went through her clothing, looking for any signs of foul treatment, I had hoped to find something similar to what I'd seen in other cases. After several minutes, I found a mark on her collarbone. There was a yellow symbol that looked just like a broken heart.

I turned to the Grand Mistress, measuring my words so I gave nothing away. "What kind of relationship was this girl in? Did she have a boyfriend who she broke up with recently?" I asked.

"Not that I was aware of. Many of the girls at that age are still in training to finish out their magical certificates. Boyfriends are usually more of a hindrance to the ultimate goal."

I traced the symbol on her skin, trying to see if it was some kind of marker. The *tvary* stayed true, and now I was curious about if there had been any marks on Alina. I'd looked at the background but hadn't checked for them on her body. Well, as much as I could find through pictures.

We needed to check on the shifter bodies as well.

I placed Flora's shirt back in place, not wanting them to ask me about seeing things. Had the *tvary* ability come from the bruja line? That would be something to look up in my mother's journals once I got out of here.

I didn't need them putting together I was Olivia Beckett or Belinda Sanchez's daughter, not while I was stuck here.

"What can you tell me about her?" I pulled out my small notebook and mini pen, ready to write some notes for later.

The Grand Mistress turned to Sage. "Help the detective. I know little about the day-to-day things in Flora's life."

The woman nodded and said, "This is Flora Cyan. She was eighteen years old and one of the most accomplished bruja in the upcoming class. She was set to graduate in a few months to the order of a full bruja." She shook her head as if she still couldn't believe this was happening. "She was very talented and reminded me of—" She stopped, glancing at the Grand Mistress, who stopped her words altogether.

"That's enough. She showed promise, that was for sure."

They were trying to hide something, I just wasn't sure what it was. "Did she have any problems with friends?" I thought of the group of friends Alina had and wondered if maybe this was a cycle every few years. One of the brightest of the upcoming group gets killed?

Something about all that brought to mind my mother's journal entry. There had been six close friends and one, Selena, had died or went away. Was it a trend I'd have to unravel?

Sage leaned up against the metal banister looming over the back bench of the theater. "She had several friends, all of whom were promising talent."

"Were?" I asked. How many more bodies would I have to investigate?

"We haven't seen them in several days. They were reported missing a day after their last sighting." Sage glanced over at the Grand Mistress, whose expression hadn't changed in minutes.

"When was this?" It was a lot more work to keep my expression neutral after receiving the information. I wondered how anyone could survive here, but it sounded like their rule about permission to leave the premises was easier to go around than the Grand Mistress had led me to believe.

Sage glanced toward the ceiling for a few seconds and then back to me. "Probably four or five days ago. We've had a group out searching for them, but they found no signs of the girls leaving the premises."

"Have you had other instances of this happening?" Man, getting info was like pulling teeth with these people.

"Not recently, no," one man said.

"I'm going to need the files or reports or whatever you people do here for all the girls."

The Grand Mistress looked unhappy. "We have a records room Sage will take you to."

My phone rang and relief shot through me at the sight of Heath's name on the screen. I needed a break from prying details from these witches.

"Did you find her?" I needed information and fast if I was ever going to leave this strange place.

"Claire, it's Stacia. The Mayor said you got a body?"

"Yeah, I do. Have you figured out anything from the other shifter bodies?"

A sound caused me to glance over at the Grand Mistress and she said, "You dare to lump us in with those dirty thieves?"

I turned and walked a few steps away, not wanting to put up with her bullshit anymore. "Hopefully Heath gave you the file we're working on from a cold case. Really, anything you have will help me at this point."

"I'm looking at one now. Tork said they found one almost identical to the one you're looking into, only this one went through our morgue," she said. I paused, waiting for her to read through it all while avoiding the stink eye of the Grand Mistress.

"Okay," Stacia said after about a minute. "It looks like the coroner at the time was a human. He didn't have any idea what would've caused this, blaming it on poisoning by some kind of acid. But from the look of the holes, I would think it would have eaten up more than just her heart and liver."

I paused, surprised. "What would only eat those organs when there are others in there?" I asked out loud.

"That's a brilliant question, but I'm not convinced it was an acid. Could they be using the organs for some kind of spell? I'm no bruja or anything," Stacia said, "But it's possible the organs were needed for something like that. Will they let me in to see the body?"

I glanced up at the two women standing before me. Lowering the phone so I wasn't talking directly to Stacia, I asked, "Will you let our coroner in to work on the body?"

The Grand Mistress shook her head even before I'd finished speaking. "Absolutely not. We have our own coroner of sorts and you can work with her."

Sage frowned and I could tell the 'of sorts' part of that answer would mean whoever the coroner was, she'd be far less trained than Stacia.

"Can I at least do a video call?" I strode over to the body and without waiting for an answer, I pressed the little button that changed our phone call over to requesting a video chat. Stacia came on the line and I turned the camera on my phone so she could see the body.

"Go closer," Stacia said, and I cringed, wondering if I would need to get a new phone after this adventure. Blood already made me squeamish, and while there wasn't a ton, I didn't need to think about it every time I picked up my phone.

"From what I can see in the dim light," Stacia said, adding a bit of sarcasm to her comment, which was another reason I liked her, "it looks like the heart is gone but the lungs are still intact, although a bit singed. Take the camera down to the other hole."

I moved the camera, hoping to find an answer with Stacia's knowledge.

"It looks like this one had her kidney taken out."

"What would cause that?" I had no idea either and glanced up at the waiting guardians staring at me from above. "Is there a spell or anything you can think of that would require a couple of parts and different organs?"

If only there was a speed course to learn more about the bruja, I would devour it like a cheeseburger. I hated the feeling of being unprepared and in the dark about anything. This was just one more reason I needed to spend more time at my mother's cottage, brushing up on things I should've learned over the past twenty-five years.

The Grand Mistress's stare was steely, and she shook her head. "We rarely use human organs for any spell."

I glanced back down at the body. The section where the burns were had little indentations that looked almost like finger marks. Had someone been able to reach through and grab the girl's organs? I shuddered, thinking of the scene in Indiana Jones and the Temple of Doom, where they stick their hand in to take out Indiana's heart.

But there had been no one next to the victim who'd seen what was happening. Would it have been possible to do it before she got into the council meeting? I shook my head, knowing it wouldn't work because the burn marks hadn't formed until I'd started doing compressions.

"Can you take me up and open her eyelids?" Stacia asked. It felt strange to open someone's eyelids, since I was usually the one closing them at a murder scene if they weren't already closed. Aside from being bloodshot, there wasn't anything off about her eyes.

"Okay, let me see her tongue." I opened Flora's mouth and turned on the flashlight on my phone so Stacia could get a better look inside. "Okay, I'll have to do some research for this one. I can do it now before I do an autopsy on the latest murder victim in Crescent City. The human side anyway."

"Will you call me with anything you find? You'll have to use Heath's phone though," I said.

"For sure. I know it's not my place, but Heath is a wreck over here," she said, a smile in her whisper.

"A wreck about what?"

"You."

I scrambled to take the phone off video and speaker so the intimidating bruja didn't hear anymore. After a few steps away from the group, I shook my head, knowing that reading too much into her comments would only make me vulnerable. "He's my protector, Stacia. Of course he's worried because he can't come onto the bruja lands right now."

There was some talking, and Heath got on the phone. "Beckett?"

My heart rate sped up. Had he heard our conversation? I hoped not. I didn't need that kind of awkwardness right now.

"I'm here."

"What did they say?"

"I'm supposed to stay here at least two weeks to find the killer. And I think their intention is to kill me if I don't get it solved."

I heard him curse under his breath. "That won't happen. You'll check in with me twice every day. Tell the Grand Mistress to expect a visit from me if you miss one of those." The protectiveness in his voice was strong, and I did all I could to make it seem like my thoughts were only on the case, since the council members were staring me down.

What did I say after that? "Got it. Just tell Stacia to call the minute she knows something."

"You're one of the best cops out there, Beckett. Figure it out."

I hung up the phone and stood, trying to figure out what to

do next. My brain kept going over his words, the phrase infusing confidence.

"Where is this coroner you talked about?" I asked. "Who do we call to move the body?"

"No need," the Grand Mistress said, flicking her wrists toward the body. The girl's body rose off the ground and floated in the air, moving with the motions of the Grand Mistress. She directed the body down the stairs, and out of the building.

I followed, wanting to make sure I knew where the body went in case I needed to inspect it for further evidence.

We stepped out into the cold winter night, and I wished I'd brought my winter coat instead of just my leather jacket. The cloak I was still wearing was thin and did little to protect me from the wind blowing through the buildings. But how was I to know I'd be here for longer than a few hours?

As I watched the Grand Mistress work, I wondered if there was a spell that could transport the body from one spot to another.

I must've said it out loud because the Grand Mistress glared at me for a few seconds before turning back to the body.

"Do you want all evidence intact?" she asked. "Teleportation breaks down the molecules to put them back together at the other place. There is never a guarantee everything will make it through the transfer."

Touché.

The building was smaller and the inside smelled as though something had been rotting for years. I glanced at the other members who'd followed us inside, but they didn't flinch at the smell.

"Does this place not get cleaned?" I muttered.

After placing the body on an open table in the first room, the Grand Mistress turned toward me, her nostrils flared in disgust. "You must be a shifter if you can smell such things.

Which shifter family do you descend from?" It was the first time I didn't see burning hatred from her when shifters were mentioned.

Trying to lie but stay close enough to the truth, I said, "I just moved here a few months ago. I'm still learning about my paranormal abilities."

The older woman gave me another once over and I wondered if she really didn't remember meeting me in the store.

"What family do you come from, Grand Mistress?" It was a chance, but learning more about her might help me gauge what else I could ask of her.

"My mother was a Tomlinson. It's close to the size of the Michaels clan." Like Levi and his sister, Stephanie, the half-bruja?

"What does the coven have to say about half-breeds?" It seemed like they kept a tight grip on their coven members but was that only for the full-blooded?

Again, Adelaide/the Grand Mistress looked me over, not amused by what I'd asked. "That's enough for today, Detective. Get to work. Two weeks isn't long to find your killer."

As she walked by me, I touched her arm and she turned around. "Have we ever met before?"

"No, but I've heard a lot about the newest detective from the PPD. And half-breeds like you have a hard time fitting into the Shadowmoon Coven."

TWENTY-THREE

I didn't have a chance to say anything before she walked out of the building, flanked by the two warlocks who were basically her bodyguards, as they hadn't said much throughout the night's events.

Well, she knew I was a half-bruja. The fact she'd said I wouldn't fit in caused every bit of my competitive side to surface, making me want to prove her wrong. But before I could do that, I needed to solve these murders.

For several seconds, I wondered if it could have been the Grand Mistress who'd orchestrated the killings. There had to be a way to cast a spell in order to remove organs from a live body in front of a full room. Just saying it sounded ridiculous.

"It's probably a good thing I don't work for her," I said to Sage, motioning toward the door.

"You wouldn't last one day under her guidance." Sage's eyes seemed to dance, as though she'd just won the fight with that quip.

I tried to keep my smile under wraps, but the corners of my lips rose. "Better to be a hunting dog than a lap one."

Sage's mouth dropped open, and she looked horrified. "If I could, I would kill you right now for speaking to me in such a manner." I noticed the small lines around her eyes and wondered how old she was. It seemed like she was trying to be younger, maybe in her thirties when she was actually in her forties.

"I really don't give a shit what you think. Right now, your coven is terrified something will come murder them, even in a large crowd. Are you willing to help me avoid a full-fledged panic?"

Sage straightened, her pose back to the perfect assistant I'd seen at the beginning of the meeting. "What do you need?"

I glanced at the time on my phone and was surprised to find it was only nine o'clock. I'd only been here an hour? That could be good or bad, since I was stuck here for a few weeks. I only hoped I'd be able to figure out what we needed to do with the bodies and the evidence.

"I'll need the files from Alina's autopsy."

Sage blinked several times, reminding me of a robot who had to be told the specific instructions the controller needed. She finally stepped to the side, walking over to a set of drawers at the far side of the room. With a small key in hand, she opened the middle drawer, pulling out an extensive file.

"This is everything we have on her death." She placed the file folder on the countertop next to me, as if she didn't want me to touch her.

I flipped through the first few pages, glancing through several photographs similar to what we'd been given at the precinct. The tension was high, and it felt awkward to have her staring at me while I went through the pages.

"Do you know Sloan?" I asked, stopping on a sheet that detailed the findings from the coroner. It differed from the ones

I usually saw from Stacia, but I'd take anything compared to the nearly blank file we'd been given.

The woman's eyes turned to me, sending a chill down my spine.

"I know most of the bruja who live in our lands." Not the most forthcoming answer, but I was going to take it as a yes.

"Alina Young, daughter of Mary Michaels. Sage Michaels, Sloan Michaels. I figured there would be a connection there. Are you a great aunt to her as well?"

Sage scowled. "Where did you hear that?"

"Funny story. Some older shifter lady made a family tree website." I grinned wider when Sage's face puckered, looking a lot like she'd just tasted the juice from a whole lemon.

"Is there any way I can speak with her? Sloan, I mean." I didn't hold out much hope, but I had to try.

"Is she connected to this case?"

I almost nodded yes, but then decided against it, giving her a small shake of the head.

"Then I suggest you stick to solving this case. It's the only reason you're allowed onto our lands. Although I detect partial bruja within you. Not that it automatically gives you a home here." She reminded me of the mean girls in high school, and I wondered what she'd gone through to be so bitter about life.

I thought about asking her what strength I was, comparing it to the rest of the bruja, but I figured I'd stay on her good side. Well, what was left of it. A lot could happen, and I didn't want to tick off the killer if I could help it. I hadn't crossed her off my list yet.

"Will this be all, Detective Beckett?" Sage asked, waving toward the open file.

"For tonight, yes. Can I take the file? To study tonight." I probably wouldn't have a TV in this place, and my phone wasn't working at full capacity. A file would help me pass the time while coming up with theories of who the killer could be.

She nodded, and we walked toward the main door. After locking it up, Sage said, "I'll show you to your room. The Grand Mistress has cleared my schedule for the morning, so think of the people you need to interview so we can get going on it first thing."

I smirked. "For being the Grand Mistress's bitch, you seem to be awfully uncomfortable helping the police."

Sage narrowed her eyes at me, sending a wave of intense hatred toward me. "A lot of good the police have done in the past."

With a slight shrug, I raised my voice and said, "Did your people even give us a chance?"

The fire in her eyes went away, and she shook her head.

"That's why we're here now. We paranormal detectives to help get things solved and to keep the peace. If you'd just stop kicking against me, you might find I'm on your side."

A stare-off ensued between us and she finally lifted her hand, pointing behind the makeshift morgue and even further from the building where the meeting had taken place.

"You'll be staying in the dorms over here."

We walked several yards, not saying much on our way to what looked like rows of housing units. I snuck glimpses of the woman walking next to me, trying to piece together who she was. She'd probably gotten her position through cunning and mind games. But why wouldn't she want to help solve her great niece's case?

"What questions do you have, Detective Beckett?" She didn't turn toward me as she asked the question.

"How long have you been the right-hand woman to the Grand Mistress?"

"Four years. I was brought in as the replacement for a woman who went missing."

A bunch of girls go missing and now she admitted to more? It seemed like they ran this place similar to an internment camp, one with poor security.

"You'll be staying here," Sage said, motioning to the building up ahead. There were no lights on and it seemed like the ultimate barracks situation. She unlocked the door and walked about halfway down the hallway before she opened another door on the left. These people were intense about their locks.

"Curfew is now," she said, standing next to the door so I could walk inside. "And some of the small cafés will be open in the morning for breakfast."

I hadn't thought I'd be staying here longer than one night and with only a set of bedclothes sitting on the bed, I wasn't sure what to do. Turning to Sage, I said, "So I have nothing else to wear. Do you have any clothing I could borrow or can I request someone to drop off a bag tomorrow?" I wondered why the bruja were so strict about comings and goings. Then again, I knew little of their history to be in a place of empathy.

"I will discuss it with the Grand Mistress," Sage said. She pinched her nose as if I were the thorn in her side. "I'll meet you tomorrow morning just outside the youth barracks, two buildings over from this one, around nine. I hope you're serious about figuring this out because I don't enjoy having my time wasted." With that, she walked out the door and slammed it shut.

Great. What the hell had I gotten myself into?

TWENTY-FOUR

Maybe I was just getting pickier in my old age, but it was one of the worst nights of sleep I'd ever had.

The sheets were scratchy and when the heating vent turned on, it sounded like someone banging a spoon inside a metal pot. I was definitely hungrier now than usual, probably because my brain thought I was being called to dinner. And when it finally turned off, giving me a break from the loud noises, I nearly froze under the thin blanket I'd been given.

I pulled my clothes back on after having slept in my bra and underwear, wishing I could take a regular shower back at my apartment. I've been grateful for it before, but never so much as I was now.

And if I ever got out of here, I was going to make sure I was always prepared with an overnight duffel bag.

I got breakfast at the commissary, surprised by how many whispers I heard as I walked by. The room had been buzzing with chatter and activity, but it was as if everyone froze once I walked into the room.

At least the coffee was good, nearly like the coffee shop I

frequented every morning near the precinct. I bought a muffin and a few granola bars. It was possible the dining services could be shut down early and I didn't want to be stranded without food.

"At least your timeliness is commendable." Sage frowned at me as she walked up to the barracks. She glanced down at the muffin in my hand and turned her nose up. "But your lack of health leaves something to be desired."

"Who shit in your cereal?" Sage's eyes went wide and her mouth dropped open as if I'd just committed a great and grievous sin. My patience had worn thin last night, and I was hoping she'd be a bit more helpful today after having laid out the reason I was here. Apparently, I was wrong.

"What are you talking about?"

"I'm talking about the bitchy attitude you keep giving me. Are you ever happy?"

She folded her arms over her chest and glared at me, but I was at least two inches taller which seemed to irk her.

"I just don't like having my time wasted," she said.

I made a humming sound and said, "I get that. I like being productive as well but do you think this is wasting your time? Looking for a killer in your midst? Don't you have any sympathy for the girl who died last night? And your great niece? She deserves justice." I'd pictured the girl's face several times as I tried to get back to sleep, usually combing over every bit and every detail of the scene in my head.

"Maybe you're the person I should look into." I stepped forward, trying to intimidate her.

She looked appalled, as if I had just taken away something she loved dearly. "I am Second on the Council of the Shadow-moon Coven Bruja. I have no reason to kill my own kind. If anyone is going to be killed, it would be me for lack of general feeling from the rest of the group."

"No surprise there," I said, taking a bite of the muffin. "Is this how the bruja are supposed to act? All stuffy and ornery all the time?"

She took a deep breath and motioned toward the main campus.

Maybe I'd been watching too many fantasy shows about witches growing up, but even with all the shit the people in the Harry Potter movies went through, they seemed to enjoy life. Everything I'd seen since stepping onto the land here was the complete opposite.

"The Grand Mistress believes in strict order. After the history we've suffered, it's the best way to live. There are no surprises that way."

"In the interest of mending fences between your coven and the rest of the paranormal community, and hopefully strengthening the bond between the Council and the PPD, what is the history you've gone through?"

Sage glanced at me for several seconds, her expression softening somewhat. "Where would you like to start, Detective?" Her tone was more amiable, but it was like she was dismissing my question.

"I'd like to speak with the mother of Flora, if possible. I need to get more information on who she was as a person, as well as understand where she'd been during the day yesterday."

"I can help you with that first part now," Sage said, pointing to a woman walking toward us. "That's Flora's mother, Bruja Cyan."

I walked up to the woman, noting the red-rimmed eyes of a woman in grief. "Hello, ma'am," I said in a soft tone, hoping not to startle her.

The woman glanced up and lifted a tissue to wipe underneath her eyes. "You must be the detective," she choked out. All the feelings she was going through reminded me of when my mother passed away and even sent me spiraling for a moment right there. There was nothing so deep as the pain felt from the death of a loved one. She was probably waffling between the idea this couldn't be happening and trying to imagine a life without her daughter.

"Yes," I said, touching her arm softly. "I'm Detective Beckett. I'm hoping to find whoever did this to your daughter."

"I hope so, too," the woman said, her voice shaky.

"Was there anything different about your daughter's behavior or activities over the last few days or weeks?"

"Not that I can think of right now. She was a lovely girl, very quiet, but she had a good group of friends."

"Sage tells me the girls have gone missing. Do you know why Flora wasn't with them?"

"There was supposed to be a celebration," the woman said, glancing up with fear at Sage. Sage stiffened, and I got the feeling celebrations weren't allowed in this section of Crescent City. "Flora kept talking about it, excited as the day got closer. But then she got really sick. She was throwing up all night before could barely stand. She was heartbroken she wouldn't be able to go, but it was better that she stayed home."

"Okay, when was this party supposed to take place?" I had my notebook out, jotting down a few details here and there so I wouldn't forget. Interviewing several people in a row could mix up the important dates and information.

"Four days ago."

"Do you have any idea where the party was to take place?"

Again, Bruja Cyan glanced over at Sage, looking more guilty. "I'm not sure the exact location."

"Even a general area will help me more than what I've got now," I said, trying to gain her trust.

Taking in a big gulp of breath, the woman said, "In the back glen there is an old barn. That's where they were supposed to go.

A quick glance at Sage told me something like this had happened before, and it was definitely off-limits. But from the strict way they had run these lands, I wasn't sure how many more bruja would want to continue following everything to the letter. From everything I'd seen so far, it was like they were toeing the line with rebellion if rules continued to tighten.

I didn't blame them. Being stuck inside here, with all the rules and do's and don'ts, wouldn't be good for my ego.

"Thank you so much," I said, giving her a small smile. "I'll make sure you know what happened once we've solved the case."

The woman walked away, her shoulders turned in and dabbing at her eyes. My heart went out to her and the urgency of finding the killer intensified.

I turned to Sage. "Tell me about this old barn as we walk toward the homes of the missing girls."

"The barn was used as the initiation into the Black Order decades ago. Many bruja like to go there to pretend they wield the power the bruja of this coven once had."

"First question: what is the Black Order? And second, what caused the power to decrease?"

Sage's jaw tightened, and I watched the indecision play in her eyes. She was definitely debating whether to share this information.

Grabbing onto my upper arm, she walked me over to a building just behind the dormitories where I'd stayed the night.

"What are you doing? Why are we going in here?" I asked, trying to roll my arm away from her. Her grip only tightened.

Once inside, what turned out to be the showers, she let go of me, walking over and turning on the water.

I was pretty sure the woman had gone crazy. What had I

said to change her demeanor? I knew I'd been harsh, but I thought we'd made some progress before she'd swung in the opposite direction.

She stepped up, leaning next to me against the wall. "The Black Order was a secret society started by some of the most powerful bruja in the coven."

"You said it was. What happened?" A secret society? It made me wonder if there was one of those in every pack and coven in the city.

"The Council could never find it, was never able to track the members, until eight or nine years ago. The Grand Mistress at the time was given information on the meeting place of the current group. When she arrived with several of her most senior bruja, she realized it was a diversion, and the Codex was stolen."

I was suddenly grateful for the running water of the shower, just in case she heard my heart beating out of my chest. My mother must've been the one to organize the heist.

"I've heard about the theft of the Codex. Has anyone located it or the thief?"

Sage glanced down at her nails and shook her head. "No one knows where the Codex is, although the Grand Mistress has every spy out searching for it. It's the reason our powers are dimming. We need the life source the Codex provides to continue to do magic."

"How long do you think you can go before your magic is extinguished completely?" There was always a possibility my mother had left the Codex among the things now stored in Heath's shed, but after finding the secret compartment, I was thinking she'd come up with somewhere that hid the book better.

"I'm not sure, but from everything I've felt in the change, I would say we only have a handful of months left."

I turned the page and began a list of cases still needing to be solved. It would probably continue to grow as the days went along here. All the disappearances and other crimes would need to be rectified.

"What are you writing?" Sage asked, peering over my shoulder.

"Just making sure it's on my list of things to solve."

Her expression was thoughtful this time. "You're going to look for the Codex?"

I shrugged, sticking the pen and notebook back into my jacket pocket. "I'm a detective and solving crimes is my job. Finding the thief and the stolen goods is just another one of those things." I pointed toward the shower. "I'm assuming you had this on to deter anyone from listening in?"

Sage nodded. "The Grand Mistress has ears everywhere."

"Do you believe everything she commands?" When she shook her head, I asked, "Then why continue to work by her side?"

"Because knowing your enemy is better than being ignorant."

TWENTY-FIVE

I might have looked like a fish after that comment. "The Grand Mistress is your enemy? In what way?" If it was true, this woman was an intense and adept actor. I'd figured she was all for everything the council decreed.

"I'm against the rules and regulations of the monarchy here. But the movement isn't ready to reveal itself yet, and I have to bide my time while I wait."

My brain ticked through all the things I'd learned from her over the past eighteen hours, flabbergasted that she'd fooled me so well. I thought about one detail, trying to make sense of it through the lens of the case I was working on.

"You've been the first assistant for four years. But three years ago was when your great niece was murdered. How have you been able to get through it?"

"Alina's mother is my niece, even though she's about ten years older than me. My father remarried after his first wife was killed, and they had me. I've always been close to Mary, and the death of Alina was a blow to their family. She'd held such promise, some people even whispering she would become the next Grand Mistress."

That could be a strike toward the current Grand Mistress. But was it motive enough to kill a young bruja?

"Did you know Alina's friends at all? Anything that could help me figure out a better lead on the killer would be helpful."

Sage nodded. "I can get you in to see them, but we have to wait until shift change to avoid detection."

As much as I wanted to trust the words, I still needed to test out what Sage said as being true.

"I have someone you can talk to who taught both girls while we wait. It will hopefully take people off the trail of where we're investigating."

Sage turned off the shower, and we walked out into the bright sunlight. There was a lot less snow here, but I was still grateful I'd worn my boots. Wet socks were the worst thing ever, and since I didn't have a second pair, I'd have to survive with what I had.

As we walked, because we walked just about everywhere, toward what looked like a school building, I figured I'd get some information on the history of the coven from her.

"Who was the coven leader before the Grand Mistress?" I asked.

"Our coven goes back centuries," Sage said. "So, there have been several. But the three before her were Rose McGregor, Shira Dawn, and Cynthia Tournos."

"What makes up a change in position?" I asked. We made it to the building, and I opened the door for Sage, getting a small smile of thanks. It was strange to see the real Sage now, not the one who was an ass-kissing loyalist to the governing body of the bruja.

"Murder or insanity."

She'd walked through the door already and I hurried my steps to walk next to her, allowing me to see her face.

"Murder? Like what we just saw with Flora?" I was understanding why my mother had fled the Shadowmoon coven. It sounded like there was more drama here than in a Broadway theater.

"Yeah, there have been poisonings and stabbings. Either of those can turn to death or make a person crazy." Sage leaned in, her voice going lower. "Cynthia Tournos basically ran into the woods and didn't come out for days. When she did, she was stark naked and thinking she was some kind of shifter. To say the coven was outraged would be an understatement."

I chuckled, remembering my comment about the shifters in the meeting earlier. "It's like the shifters have the plague or something."

We both laughed for several steps. The hallway we walked down was dim, but some sun shone through the windows above us. We walked past several classrooms, and I realized this must be where all the young kids studied magic.

It was tempting to step in and listen for a while, wondering what I would pick up in the process. I wouldn't even mind the boring classes because it might help me understand this world more.

"Why don't we have any files of these types of killings?" I asked, irritated that she hadn't answered my question. I was here to do a job, not just hang out in the same clothes I'd worn yesterday and jump through all their hoops.

"Because the Grand Mistress worries about having outsiders in our midst all the time will take our powers away faster. The coven has its own way of handling deaths, mostly just sweeping them under the rug and continuing on with life."

"What changed? Why allow me to come in now?" I asked, hoping to get a bigger picture of all this.

"Because it was part of the agreement the Grand Mistress made with Heath Langton a few weeks ago. We were to work with the police department on anything out of the ordinary and anything criminal, and he would allow three of the twelve Crescent City Council seats to be occupied by members of the bruja."

"Only three?" I wrinkled my nose, surprised by the negotiation. Had Heath messed that one up?

"The only other group with that number is the shifter pack, meaning if there's a deal we don't like, we can come to a stalemate." Sage leaned closer to me and said, "I'm surprised he gave in that much as it is."

I nodded, feeling the same. "It isn't like him to give up something if he can see it has potential to go sideways. Let's just hope he knows what he's doing." The two groups together would make up half the vote if they all voted the same.

I couldn't help but grin. "It will probably take some getting used to then, huh?"

Sage nodded, looking somewhat worried about it. "There are things the Grand Mistress won't even discuss with us. I don't know who she confides in completely, but I'm wary of whatever plans she's coming up with."

She walked up to a door on the left side and opened it. The voices in the room quieted down some as Sage strode over and spoke with the teacher, a very young woman, who seemed young enough she could've still been a student.

The classroom was filled with boys and girls, all of them wearing uniforms of black, purple, and gray. It seemed I was the most exciting person in the room and every eye was staring at me.

I gave a half-wave, not sure if it was another thing I wasn't allowed to do in this part of the city. So many rules, but it seemed I'd broken most of them already.

The teacher stood and said, "Please practice the levitation incantation while I'm gone. And do not lift any of your class-mates. I'm looking at you, Johnny Burns." The group gave a soft chuckle, as if even laughing were prohibited.

The teacher followed Sage out of the room and into the hallway.

Sage gestured to her and said, "This is Rachel Frank. She taught both Alina and Flora." Sage leaned up against the wall, studying her fingernails and looking like she'd rather be anywhere else. How she could transform back into the sullen character so quickly, I'd never know.

I guess I was on my own to interrogate this woman.

"You taught both girls," I said, trying to come up with a thoughtful question. "Were there any similarities between the two of them?"

Rachel gave me a sad smile and nodded. "Yes, both girls were bright. They understood a lot of the harder concepts early, but were both very shy, almost to the point of it being painful when they were called on to do anything."

I had little experience with it, but I'd known a few people in my high school who'd been that way. Eunice, a victim of Lee Vance, was just like that. But if Alina was so quiet, why would she be seen as the future Grand Mistress? Leading an entire coven of bruja would take leadership skills, and if someone couldn't command, it wouldn't matter how powerful she was.

"Okay, and their groups of friends. I've heard in both cases there were five or six girls who ran around together. Is there anything you can tell me about them?"

I hoped her friends would give me more insight into what had been going on. But right now, the ones who'd been friends with Alina weren't able to speak, and the ones who were friends with Flora had gone missing. So many pieces and I wasn't sure I'd be able to find them all in two weeks' time, especially if I didn't have help from my team. Yeah, I was strong enough to admit it.

"Both groups had a good mixture of girls and talent. There were a few of the top bruja and some who struggled with classes."

"Was there anything suspicious you can remember a few days before their deaths?" It wasn't my strongest question ever, but we'd solved cases with a small clue, and I was hoping to have that too.

Rachel shook her head before stopping, her eyes riveted on something across the hall. I turned, finding nothing but the dingy carpet used in most high schools.

"There was something strange, now that I think of it. Both times, one girl in the group had acted out in either a class or in the cafeteria. Full-on writhing and acting possessed. I only heard about Truvy, a friend of Alina's doing it in the classroom, but about four days ago, Laura, Flora's friend, fell down in the cafeteria with spasms."

Sage had straightened, looking a bit more interested in the conversation now. "Were the incidents reported?"

Rachel shrugged. "I'm not sure. I was only passing through the cafeteria when it happened with Laura. I had to get back to the classroom to get ready for the students to return."

I noticed the way Rachel avoided looking directly into Sage's eyes and wondered how much power this bruja truly had when it came to the day-to-day tasks of the coven.

"How many students attend this school?" I asked, curious as to the number put into each class. "And are they based on age or talent?"

"We have six hundred in the junior school, with another five hundred and fifty in the senior school. There are certain classes only taught by age level and then a few select classes are allowed to go by talent."

I tried to cram all of it into my brain. Rachel had said the groups the two girls had run around in were a mixture of talents, meaning they could have only been introduced to one another in the age level classes. But wouldn't the talent class be a better place to form a friend group? Or allies, perhaps?

I nodded. "Thank you, Rachel. I'll let you know if I have more questions."

Rachel smiled at me, looking a bit more relaxed than when she'd first stepped out into the hall. With a nod, she headed back into the classroom, calling out orders the minute she passed through the door.

Sage raised her eyebrows. "Where to next, Detective?"

"To see the silent girls."

TWENTY-SIX

I wasn't completely sure what I was getting myself into. To be honest, I hoped I'd be the magic key who could unlock the silence of the girls and get all the details I needed for this case.

But once we'd stepped into the large room, with dim lights shining overhead, I realized this was going to be more difficult than I'd thought. The room had two benches in it, facing a large glass wall that seemed to be cut up into what looked like cells. A woman was inside each of them, either laying on the cot or sitting on a chair. Their long hair covered most of their features, but the pale skin tones of each told me none of them had seen the sun in a long time.

"Why are they being kept here?" I asked, having noted the sanatorium sign as we'd walked into the building. It was several minutes from the school, tucked behind a grove of pine trees. The whole bruja lands had been covered with different varieties of trees, but these were thicker and a lot closer together than the others, as if they were trying to help the rest of the coven forget the building was even there.

"For their safety. Several of them have tried to cut themselves, or other manners of suicide." Sage shook her head, looking as though she couldn't help the girls.

"I want to go inside," I said, stepping over to a door that looked to be normal, until I touched the handle. A shock wave of heat flooded through my palm but it still took several seconds for my brain to process the heat. By the time I flinched back, my palm was a bloody, charred mess.

"Why didn't you warn me about it?" I said.

"I didn't think you'd go grabbing the handle," Sage said, stepping over to the wall next to the door. She took a small key from her breast pocket and turned it into the lock at the side of the door. I could hear the mechanism clicking, but I still was hesitant to touch it.

The pain seeping through my hand was excruciating as the cells knit themselves back together.

Thank you, Dad, wherever you are, for self-healing.

I wasn't sure what I would've done if my body didn't heal itself every time I was injured now. The real question was why it hadn't done it with the gunshot wound to my thigh. Did I have to be in Crescent City in order for the healing to work? Or was it this place had triggered my abilities?

I clenched my teeth together, hoping to hide the pain racking my body. Sage watched with curiosity, her eyes wide as the last few pieces of flesh moved into place, the callouses and palm now smooth with no evidence anything had ever happened.

"Shifter, huh?" she asked, curiosity brimming in her eyes.

"Partial. But the whole healing thing is a nice benefit."

Sage nodded. "I can imagine so, especially in your line of work. I had a friend once who was a half-breed. They sent her to another section of the bruja lands the first time she shifted."

"What is it with the bruja? Why can't they accept the halflings?" Maybe I was asking for my own benefit, but I wanted to know what the real beef was between the two groups.

With a sigh, Sage said, "The bruja were the originals here in Crescent City. Our coven established the paranormal community, helping those without covens and packs to find their place. But things changed, probably twenty-five years ago. There was so much in-fighting it was hard to keep hold of the power in the city. That's when the shifters started running things."

"Do you think they've done a good job?" I inhaled, feeling back to normal after the trauma of the burned palm.

Sage nodded. "I don't think they've done an awful job, but having more people to voice opinions about the distinct groups would be better."

I stepped through the door and turned to Sage. "I'd like to speak with them alone, please."

Sage nodded. "Let me get a clip of their cells right now for several seconds and I'll run it on a loop."

With a quick nod, I waited for her signal before I walked back to the cells.

I was about to head toward the first room, when I turned and glared back at her. "All the other systems have been shut off, right? No more burning limbs?"

What would I have done without her help? There was so much I didn't know about this place, but Sage had navigated most things. I still suspected her quick change in attitude, but I'd just watch for any signal I was in trouble.

Sage blinked and nodded. "Everything has been turned off."

At that response, I headed toward the first room, glancing down at my palm. The skin looked perfect, but it was like what remained hadn't been long enough to stretch back in place. The tightness when I spread my fingers open made me wonder if it would go back to normal after a certain time period. I hoped it would.

The gift of self-healing was great in theory, but it hurt like hell, something I hadn't realized from my initial ankle break since I'd been given such high pain killers. I knocked on the glass door of the first cell and waited for the girl to respond. It took three different knocks before she even looked through the glass door at me.

"May I come in?" I asked, using my pointer finger to point at her.

Without moving, the door latch gave way, and the door swung open with more force than if I'd just gently pushed it.

I hesitated, wondering if I'd be able to open the door to escape if it accidentally shut once I was inside. A quick glance through the opposite window, the one I could see when we first walked in, told me Sage was sitting on a bench, watching every move I made in the cell. Hopefully she'd be there to help should anything happen.

"I'm Detective Claire Beckett. I've come to talk to you about Alina. What's your name?"

I stood awkwardly next to her. The girl had raven black hair that would probably go down to her ass when she stood up. Instead of speaking, the girl pointed to a section on the concrete floor.

Truvy was scratched out into the concrete.

"Hi Truvy. I'm here to talk to you about your friend's death. Is there anything you can tell me about her?"

Several moments of silence passed, and the girl didn't move from her spot. Instead of opening her mouth, she held out her hand, made into a fist.

I took a step forward, a slip of panic coursing through me as I wondered if she'd throw me up against the wall with her magic. I reached out, touching her fist with the tip of one finger, and jumped back a step when her fingers opened wide, revealing a small coin.

"Do you want me to take it?" I asked, not wanting to disrupt this girl's stasis here in the room.

She tipped her hand to the side and let the coin slip into my palm. It was bigger than I'd thought, a cat printed in the lower corner on the backside, along with a large book.

On the flip side, there were what looked like dots all the way around it.

"What is this for?" I asked, trying to gauge what the coin meant. "Does this connect to Alina?"

One slow blink was all I got, but I took it as a sign it connected somehow to the murder of her friend.

I took one step forward, trying to hand her back the coin. Instead of taking it, Truvy scrambled back on the bed, curling up as much as possible in the corner. The speed at which she'd done it scared me, sending my heart rate through the roof.

"Can I take this and bring it back to you when I've solved the case?"

Silence again, but I stepped backward, hoping she'd decide not to zap me with her mind magic.

I made it outside the cell and stepped to the next one, taking a few breaths before I knocked on the door. The emotions running through me were so up and down, I would be ready for a nap by dinnertime.

I went to every room, glancing out the window as Sage watched me the whole time. But each girl had something to give me, and they'd all scratched their names into the concrete, just like Truvy had.

By the time I walked out, I'd collected a coin, half of a button, two small sticks, a piece of fabric, and what looked like a small piece of glass.

I stepped into the main room, trying to figure out what they could mean. I might not have gotten them to speak, but I did manage to get whatever these things were.

"Looks like a lot of junk," Sage said, standing from the bench. "Is that what they gave you?"

"Yeah," I said, still glancing down at the pieces. "Does any of this mean something to you? Were they things Alina's family might have used?"

Sage glanced back down at my palm, reaching forward to pick up the piece of glass in one hand and the two sticks in another. She shook her head and placed them back in my hand. "I'm trying to think if there were any spells that might have used these objects, but if there is, it's dark magic. Not something I would know."

I puzzled over it for a few more seconds when she said, "Are you ready to go? The shift will change again soon." She walked over and pressed a few buttons. All the humming I'd heard from the door when I burned my hand reactivated.

"Yeah, I should be good for now."

We walked toward the main door and just before I walked outside, I turned, surprised to see all the girls were standing next to the glass, their right hand touching it. They were staring at me, and it took a few seconds for my heart to stop pounding in my chest.

"Find her." I glanced around, wondering if Sage was the one who'd spoken, but she was already out the door.

"Find her."

The words came again, only this time in my mind and in chorus.

I nodded.

I wasn't sure who they were referring to, but there was something about this case that needed to be solved and now.

TWENTY-SEVEN

I sat in the room I'd been assigned to sleep in, not excited about another night here. What I would give to be back in my apartment, or even staying at the cottage. Instead, I sat here, staring at the contents on the table in front of me.

My phone rang, the only number that seemed to work on this side of the city appearing on the screen.

"Mr. Mayor," I said, half-smiling as I waited to hear what he'd say.

"I thought we were friends, Beckett. And you come at me with that."

"It feels more official. I think they bugged this place for everything and anything."

"How's it going there? Is there something we can do to help out here?" Back to business and normally, I would be bugged, but this time, I was ready to get the hell out of the bruja lands.

"I'm going to send you a picture of five items. If you can run it through the computer or whatever, we need a hit on something." I thought about the girls I'd just visited. How had they been able to stand if they hadn't done so while I was in there?

"Okay, I've talked to the Grand Mistress and if you need anything else, just call me. I might even get Stacia in there."

I shook my head, remembering the threats the Grand Mistress had already issued against any others on my team entering the bruja lands. "I don't know if she'd be able to tell much more right now. We just need to figure out what these items mean for the murder of Alina."

"Are you okay in there?" Heath asked, his voice almost reverent. "You're not trapped or imprisoned, right?"

As much as I wished I could come up with something sarcastic to cut through the intimacy of the moment, the other part of me savored it. I'd never had a guy worry about me, even if it was just for a job.

"I'm fine. I've got a room. I could use a few clothes and some shower supplies, though." I cringed, thinking of Heath walking around my bedroom, loading things into a bag for me. And him seeing my underwear? It seemed like too much for our current relationship. "You know, if Nina isn't there, don't worry about it. I, uh, I'll be fine until we find the killer."

Heath chuckled, that deep laugh I couldn't help but smile at. "You think you'll survive a week in the one outfit you're wearing right now?"

I thought about it, knowing I didn't smell like roses at the moment. "I'd probably die if I went that long. Or flies will swarm me. Just tell Nina, or Stacia, to grab some things for me."

"Done. I'll send those over in the morning." The silence lasted a few seconds on the phone. "Beckett, stay safe."

The call ended and I might have glanced at the screen a bit longer, thinking through our conversation once again. As much as I'd fought liking him, it was probably inevitable. But did he feel the same?

I turned off the light, my brain still going a hundred directions, trying to understand the connection to the items and the murder.

Sage couldn't think of any suspects she thought would have committed the murder, and I felt like after an entire day of searching, I was still at square one with this investigation.

A sound knocked against the window, and I froze, trying to figure out what might have happened. There had been no wind blowing when I'd gotten into the room an hour earlier. Laying back down, I tried to see anything outside the window, but the moon had only been a thumbnail tonight and it wasn't as bright as usual.

The knock sounded again, and I threw off the thin blanket, walking over to the pane of glass. I'd decided to sleep fully clothed tonight, hoping I wouldn't freeze and knowing Heath would send clean clothes the next morning.

I pressed my hands against the glass, hoping to get a look at anything on the ground next to the building.

I was fully supporting my weight against the glass when it seemed to evaporate and I went tumbling out and onto the thick snow below. It could've been worse. At least this way I had a soft cushion instead of bashing my head against a rock.

Rustling sounded behind me and I whipped my head back and forth, hoping to find something, anything that would alert me to what was happening. With only socks on my feet, I didn't feel the security of using my legs to kick at anyone. But going to bed with shoes on was not my idea of comfort.

A cloth covered my mouth, gagging me. As a covering went over my eyes, I tried to pull it away, only to be pulled back by several hands, cold metal tying my wrists together.

Someone lifted me up, holding onto my wrists while guiding me through the woods.

I tried to fight against the binds, knowing my chances for

survival of a kidnapping were a lot better if I did it right now, only minutes after the initial attack.

Whoever was next to me didn't speak, but I could hear several steps and the rustle of clothing. A skirt, perhaps? Or maybe a cloak? They seemed to be all the rage here in bruja land.

I'd never had that sensation before, the amplified sound of things around me, and I wondered if my powers only worked when I was under threat, or when the fight-or-flight response kicked in.

Would my electricity be able to blast them?

I dug deep, trying to summon it. Why didn't I have a way to channel it? That's what I should've been doing at the cottage the day before coming here. Learning magic was more useful than my heritage, although I wouldn't have known the electric power came from being an elemental, or a partial one.

Nothing, not even a flicker of magic came through my arms to my wrists.

I used a finger to trace along the binds behind my back and realized they'd used magic prohibiting cuffs. I'd seen them on Lyra when she was being taken into the station after we'd arrested her. Gonzalez had explained what they were.

Well played, whoever it was.

We walked for at least a minute, and then I heard the soft purr of an engine.

Whoever had been guiding me pushed on my upper back, sending me falling against a leather cushion of sorts. My shin slammed against the bottom of a door, causing a shot of pain to travel up to my knee. I let out a cry, but the person just shoved me in leaving me the rest of the way, laying on the backseat. At least the seat was cushioned.

My head spun as a headache engaged again, rendering me unable to comprehend much more of what was happening.

I took several slow breaths, channeling my energy to relaxation rather than tensing up even more. The wave of pain subsided and it was like my sensitivity to hearing heightened again.

The motion of the car came to me. Now was the time to react. My legs weren't bound, probably so whoever had captured me wouldn't have to carry me. That meant my attacker was smaller than me to some degree.

I pulled my knees to my chest, slamming my feet against the door. The impact sent a shock wave of energy up through my legs, but all I heard was a little clang of metal. Otherwise there was no change in sound of the air in the cab.

Winding up, I pulled back again, kicking over and over, getting more desperate with each attempt. My legs tingled, like after doing a bunch of squats on leg day. I'd have to start upping my weights if I couldn't escape something like this.

I made a last attempt. This time the door released below my feet, allowing a breeze to course through the cab.

Wriggling as much as possible, I got down to where my ankles were hanging outside the vehicle.

And just as hope flooded me I might make it out, something hit me on the head, turning the world black.

TWENTY-EIGHT

My tongue was thick and dry, and my throat raw and scratchy. I blinked a few times, surprised the blindfold had been removed. The gag still covered my mouth, but at least I was sitting in a regular chair and not hooked up to any major torture devices or IVs of drip fluid. Maybe I needed to stop watching crime dramas.

With my hands bound behind me, I thought I'd have an opportunity to break free. The magic cuffs were gone but even with a big tug, my hands didn't move much.

A light flicked on in the corner, causing me to blink even more against the brightness of it.

"Why are you here?" The voice was distorted and low, sounding like the kidnappers had played it through one of those scrambler machines kidnappers used to talk to people for their ransom.

I tried to speak, still stuck against the bind around my mouth. Hands fumbled with the tie at the back and I turned, hoping to see what my kidnapper looked like.

The light turned off, and the room behind me was pitch

black. I thought if I gave my eyes some time to adjust, I'd be able to see shadows, but seconds passed and I saw nothing.

"I'm here to investigate the murder of Alina Young."

"What's your name?"

I frowned, frustrated I'd let myself get into this mess. So much for being a good detective. How was it I hadn't taken adequate precautions to guard myself from getting caught? Then again, I was turning in for the night. But in a strange area, I should've at least been on guard for anything.

When the voice repeated the question, I barked out, "What's yours? Who are you? If you want answers from me, I need answers from you."

"We are the Black Order."

"The what?" I asked, hoping to see something I could use to stall whatever torture tactics they had in store for me. Sage had said the Black Order was a secret society, just no longer active.

"We've been tasked with saving the Shadowmoon Coven from themselves. Why are you here?" I'd always thought the idea of a secret society was cool, but to be trapped with one right now, I had mixed emotions.

"I'm Detective Claire Beckett. We've had several murders lately and I've just come to investigate, hoping to find an answer and put away a killer."

Silence filled the room, and I took a deep breath in, preparing myself for some kind of attack.

"Where do you come from?"

"From Boston and most recently, Luna Avenue. Why did you bring me here? All I want to do is find the killer so I can go home."

"What have you found so far?" The voice wasn't as deep this time, and I tried to pinpoint where it was coming from. Probably to the right of me.

"Only small objects from Alina's friends in the sanitorium."

"What were the objects?"

I pictured the five things on my small desk in the empty room, triggering the memory of Heath's call. I hadn't thought to grab my phone or put my shoes on. And now I was going to miss out on the new clothes Heath was going to send me in the morning. Then again, I wasn't sure what this group had in store for me.

Death wouldn't work for me.

The lights turned on, but the room was empty, aside from me sitting in the chair. The walls were all white, and now they looked almost like I was in a padded cell.

Had I lost my shit that badly? Was I really in a mental institution?

I hoped it wouldn't end up being like the cells Alina's friends were housed in.

No one entered the room and released me. My wrists were sore already, and I wondered how long I'd been here. At least I'd be able to see if Lee Vance was coming now, right? Because all my worst nightmares were taking place right now.

A picture flashed on the screen, a puzzle with shapes.

"What do you want?" I screamed, ready for some answers. I hadn't felt such a need to know everything when I was in Boston, but now that I was here, answers sounded more like water after a desert, and I was severely dehydrated.

I stared at the puzzle again, seeing how to solve it by moving one square to another section, creating a new number.

"Move the bottom square to the right."

The box I'd mentioned shifted over, a big green check mark covering the screen. I guess it was quiz time.

Another box popped up. This time it was a scene. There were several trees and a couple of animals. I let my gaze run all over the picture, knowing I'd have to answer a question about it.

The scene disappeared, and the voice said, "How many shifters did you see?"

Four multiple choice answers appeared, and I guessed five.

A red X covered the screen and a high-pitched squealing sounded. I wasn't able to shield my ears because of the restraints, and the headache I'd had before struck me so hard I couldn't move. I gritted my teeth against it, hoping at any moment the sound would cease. But it didn't, and the pain became so intense, I closed my eyes and lost consciousness.

WHEN I CAME TO, my body felt like it had been hit with something hard, as if an invisible boulder had gone sailing through the air. I winced and wheezed, hoping to get my breath, gasping for any bit of air possible.

The screen popped up again, the same scene from before playing like a movie against the wall.

This time I answered correctly the number of rocks in the scene.

The screen changed again, numbers counting down from twenty, and then a bright light from above shined directly at my face once it was at zero. It didn't matter how much I moved my face, the light seemed to be just as bright in that new section. The stress of the light made my heart pump faster and I couldn't catch my breath again.

What in the hell was this kind of torture? Maybe I'd been expecting water or physical pain from a large hammer, but this was more psychological.

The siren rang out again, and I focused on a small tear in the fabric against the wall, breathing in and out in long breaths. This time, instead of passing out, I was at least able to remain conscious. But the stabbing pain in my head made it difficult to concentrate on anything else.

You've got this, Claire. You've been through crazy things before. This is just a test.

At least I hoped it was just a test. What if they were reprogramming my brain with all this nonsense? I couldn't worry about it right now. I just needed to stay awake so I could figure out how to get out of here. That little rip in the wall was the one thing keeping me from losing consciousness.

I wondered, in an entire room that had been meticulously put together, why they hadn't fixed the spot, and who had torn it in the first place.

Had the last person in here ripped it hoping to get out? I turned my head as much as possible, grateful the blaring noise had gone silent. There was no sign of a door. The ceiling looked completely uniform as well, and I relaxed back into the chair, checking for any abnormalities in the design.

Minutes ticked by and I heard and saw nothing on the screen. By sheer luck, I noticed a small circle disrupting the diamond pattern on the ceiling. It was over in the right corner of the room, but I figured I'd be able to rig something to reach it, if they ever took my handcuffs off.

My stomach was at the subdued hunger stage. I must have missed a few meals but didn't know if it was day or night or how long I'd been here.

"Hello?" I said, my voice hoarse from yelling the last time I'd said anything. "What do you want from me?"

Silence lasted for several seconds.

I needed to focus and figure out what they could want from me. They were the Black Order, the group Sage had spoken of in passing. Did she know they were still operational as a secret society? Or had she really believed they were done?

I was still trying to figure her out, trying to understand how the Black Order and the regular Shadowmoon Council fit together.

The facts I had were few, but any spark could help the fire burn.

Alina and Flora were both eighteen when they were murdered. They both had four or five good friends who they hung out with. Alina's group stopped hanging out a week or two before her birthday. Flora didn't make it to a celebration at the barn in the woods because she was sick.

Did it mean Flora's friends might still be at the barn? Or was that a decoy for where they were taken?

Alina's friends were all mute now. They had to have been hexed or something. Had I read about a specific hex that could silence someone? I tried to remember the situations from the books I'd gone through, but nothing came to mind.

The siren blared again. This time pain surged through the back of my head and down into my neck, making it hard to move. I had the sensation everything within me was being squeezed and as panic set in, a burn rolled through my forearms, igniting the electricity in my hands. I yanked at the restraints and they broke, sending relief through my arms.

I held the cuffs in my hand, the metal singed and still hot from the energy. Taking my chair, I slid it underneath the circle and stood on my tiptoes, barely touching the ceiling. It wasn't enough to press the button in and so I jumped, missing and jamming my thumb into one of the diamond pieces that didn't move.

I cursed and tried again, this time giving enough push to hear the movement of the tiles above, opening a large diamond shaped hole. From my angle, I could only see cords and what looked to be electrical equipment. Maybe it was connected to all the video cameras they had in this place?

The click of a door opening caused me to turn my head

weakly toward it. Three figures in black cloaks charged over to me and I jumped, hoping to lift myself up and into the attic area. I hung from the ceiling for a second as I swung my legs, trying to get the momentum to swing up into the attic or whatever was above. My feet connected with the head of one of the figures, the high-pitched squeal not coming close to what I'd already endured in here.

On my next backswing, I almost had it, but didn't realize until too late that one of the figures had gotten behind me, pulling my legs down so hard that I lost my grip and landed face first on the ground.

Blood pooled below me, and feeling the tender area of my nose, I knew I'd broken it.

"Why the hell are you torturing me? You know you'll be indicted for assaulting an officer, right?" I pushed up, using my left hand more since the right was weaker. Probably another broken bone.

Blood continued to gush out of my nose, and I didn't have anything but my shirt to clean it with. The bright red against the white floor was such a contrast, and for the hundredth time today, or whatever day it was, I wished I was back at the precinct or in my apartment.

The siren blared again and with the weakness of my body and lack of blood, I fell back toward the ground, unable to avoid the pool of blood.

TWENTY-NINE

I didn't know how long I'd been out this time, but the metallic taste in my mouth didn't help as I woke up with dried blood all over my sleeves. From a stretch of my jaw, I realized there was blood on the side of my face, and it too was dry.

Breathe in through my nose, out through my mouth.

My stomach was ready to give up whatever was left within it, probably bile at this point. I hated the sight of blood.

Rolling over, I glanced up at the ceiling. The opening from before had been closed, and I felt a sliver of defeat worming its way into my chest. I had to fight it, though. I would get out of this, or my team would find me. I had to hang onto that.

The click of a door opening caused my senses to shift back to the detective instincts inside me. I pushed to a sitting position, spinning around to glance at the figure coming near me. There was a slight hitch in her step, a hesitation that had to have been from seeing me covered in blood.

The figure removed her hood, revealing a young woman, probably eighteen or nineteen. Her white blonde hair stood out as different from most of the bruja I'd met since I'd been in the Shadowmoon Coven lands. I think I'd only seen a few sandy blonde types, but this was some other level stuff.

"Who are you?" She came to a stop just a foot in front of me, looking like she'd been trying to figure out the answer to that question for a long time.

"I'm Claire Beckett. I'm a detective for the Crescent City Paranormal Police Department." It had been a while since I'd said it all out loud, making it feel like quite a mouthful to say.

"But you're also part bruja."

She didn't mean it as a question and I stayed silent, curious what this was leading to, and how she knew it. I'd had several people tell me they could only figure out a certain part of my magical signature, and it seemed this girl was trying to do the same.

"What coven are you from?"

"I'm still trying to figure it out completely, but from everything I've found so far, my mother was a part of the Shadowmoon Coven."

"Your mother's name?" The girl's precise speech was something I'd never experienced, as if she'd been trained to speak that way for many years. But she couldn't have been much older than a high schooler.

"Olivia Beckett."

The girl went still, her expression thoughtful, probably trying to call up a picture of the woman I mentioned.

"What connections have you found within the Shadowmoon Coven then?"

Reaching out a hand, I said, "Look, I've told you who I am. The least you could do is tell me who you are or better yet, why the hell I'm here."

Silence was all I could hear for nearly a minute, but the

stubbornness inside me wouldn't budge, meaning I wouldn't ruin the chance to learn more. If I knew their motivation, I might find an escape, or even talk my way out of this.

"Hannah Kindale. Assistant to the head of the Black Order."

Two thoughts came to mind when she said that. Why did I keep ending up with the assistant to the governing leader? And how old were the rest of the women in this society?

"Who is the leader?" Chances of it being answered were slim, but I needed something to tie it all together.

The door opened again, and this time, instead of only one figure, there were at least a dozen who filed through the door and into the room. All were covered in black cloaks and I'd never been more ready to be done with them. I didn't like the anonymity it gave these people, who'd been torturing me for way too long.

"I'm the leader," one of the hooded figures said, shifting the hood back. Her face looked familiar, but I couldn't place from where. She stared at me for several seconds and a myriad of emotions ran across her face. "Belinda?"

I blinked several times, surprised she'd pinpointed my mother's actual name. "Claire." I kept my mouth shut after, knowing my best way to get answers was to let her talk.

"Take her to the room and clean her up. I want to speak with her."

These people definitely got an F for hosting.

Two of the hooded figures walked toward me, lifting me to my feet and pushing me toward the door. Outside, I almost sighed at the dimness of the light in the hall. It was soothing to my brain, and I was ready for another nap. But first I needed to get myself out of here.

The fact the leader knew who my mother was could go two

ways. Either Belinda Sanchez had slighted her, meaning I would receive more torture treatments, or my mother had helped the leader and maybe I'd be released. I just hope it was the latter.

THIRTY

They took me to a room and gave me a gray t-shirt and a pair of black sweats. My first change of clothing in how long?

After washing off the dried blood everywhere and basically giving myself a sponge bath, I dressed in the clean clothing, folding up my others and still donning the leather jacket. Who knew how long I'd be stuck in whatever room I had to be in, and I didn't want to be cold. If only they'd thought to give me some clean socks.

The two figures waited for me to leave the room, and I walked into what looked almost identical to the interrogation rooms at the CCPD. They pushed me into the room and left, clicking the door shut.

Yay for being stuck in another square room. At least this one was more forest green than stark white.

Several minutes passed, and the door opened, revealing the woman who'd called herself the leader.

Before she said anything, she slid a picture across the table where it rested right in front of me. It was the picture of my mother and her three friends, the picture in my locket. I pressed my hand against the collar of the t-shirt, making sure no part of the locket was visible before I leaned over the table to look more carefully at the picture.

There was my mother's bright smile and younger face. Next to it was who I'd thought to be Adelaide, but I now knew as Eleanor, the Grand Mistress of the Shadowmoon Coven. And there, on the end, with her eyes squinted against the sun, was a younger version of the woman standing before me.

"You knew her." I kept the awe out of my voice, but my insides were humming with the possibilities of more information, from someone I hoped would be a more credible source.

She nodded. "Oh, I knew her. We were practically inseparable, she and I."

"Do you mind telling me your name?" It was like a full dental procedure here with how little information they let me extract. I was so sick of it that adding the anesthesia with a little politeness was probably the only way to make progress.

"Raery Barker. Belinda and I grew up together and went through every level of hell possible."

Chills filtered through me. Even though the circumstances were strange, I'd finally found someone who knew enough about my mother to tell me all the details.

"What happened between you two and the other women in this picture? What are their names?" I was curious what she would say, hoping it would put a lot of things into perspective.

She pointed to the girl I knew as Adelaide. "This is Eleanor Adelaide. You've met her as the Grand Mistress. And this is Mary Michaels."

It threw me for a second and I leaned closer, noting Mary's lips and eyes were the same. She and Eleanor hadn't aged quite as well as Raery, making them look at least ten years older than her.

"So, the four of you were really close. What happened?"

Raery sat down in the chair, staring at me for several moments, as if committing my face to memory. "The four of us grew up together. Addie, who we called Adelaide, was always a straight arrow. We got into a lot of trouble one summer after taking off with a supply of new herbs that had been shipped in. This was back when the bruja ruled the paranormal world in Crescent City."

Her eyes misted over and I wanted to reach over and shake her, hoping to get every ounce of information from her while I was here. To be honest, I was waiting for Heath to come knocking down the door to find me and knew once he was here, the bruja would shut up like clams.

"Addie wasn't happy about it but didn't tell on us, which we were grateful for. Belinda and Mary would have been banished to another coven if they'd been found out. Their grandmother was someone you didn't cross."

"Were they sisters?" My mother had never mentioned a sister, but anything was possible at this point.

Raery scrunched her nose, looking as though she was trying to remember. "Second cousins, maybe? There are a lot of Michaels in the Shadowmoon Coven. Your mom invited me to a family reunion once and it seemed at least three-fourths of the coven was there. I think her mother was a Michaels."

I blinked several times, the weight of this truth settling over me. We'd lived as though we didn't have any family, no other support system in the world, and come to find out I had a large extended family. Perhaps the Black Order leader saw the hope in my eyes because she gave me a sad smile.

"There are quite a few who still live on bruja lands but wait a while before you visit. Things weren't left in the best situation once your mother moved away."

"Okay, tell me everything. I've been trying to figure out where she was from and why she never told me about any of this." Where did I even begin? The birth certificates? Or the Codex?

"I can understand that. Imagine my surprise to find you as the detective when I walked into our light room." That's what they called it? It definitely was full of blinding lights.

I nodded. "I'm just happy to be alive."

Raery smiled. "Your mother was something. One of the best people in the world, the most selfless too. All she did to save the coven is something I wish more bruja could understand."

I slid forward, waiting on every word. Since I'd arrived in Crescent City, there had been plenty of rumors of the bad things my mother had done. To find someone with whom she was close growing up, and to hear she wasn't an awful human being helped settle the lingering anxiety.

"Well, for starters, she was the head of the Black Order."

Words couldn't describe the shock settling into my chest. "Really?"

Raery nodded, smiling at me. "She was the one who helped turn it around, making the focus on the overall cause instead of self-serving magic. I took over after she left for good. A year before she was killed."

"My mom was still the head of a secret society until the year before she died?" How had she been able to hide that much from me?

"It was tricky, but she could get in and out of the Shadow-moon Coven lands fairly easily toward the end. I see signs of her all the time when I'm traveling through those passages."

"Okay, are there any members of the coven you suspect? Anyone with a vendetta against the Black Order?"

Raery placed her hand on her lap, picking a piece of string off the pant leg. "We have many haters, but few who know the details of the Order or the members."

"What about the Grand Mistress? You were close back in the day. What did she say about you becoming part of the secret society without her?"

"We never told her we were part of it. As difficult as it was, we had to distance ourselves slowly to make sure no one ever learned our secret. There are inner workings of the coven that won't help the overall cause of the bruja. That's what we're trying to stop."

I glanced over at the picture again. "What about Mary? How did they both take you not hanging out with them anymore?"

"Both had a hard time with it, especially Mary, since she's related to your mother." She blew out a long breath and said, "We were in our last year of school. Belinda and I were given a special card, slipped into our jacket pockets, inviting us to join a party. Addie and Mary weren't invited, and the oath at the induction ceremony made us promise not to tell anyone outside the Black Order about the society or its purposes."

"And yet, here I am," I said, putting my arms out, palms up, like I was making a grand entrance.

"Yes, but you're a means to an end. The key to proving our innocence in these matters."

I frowned, not sure I enjoyed being used. "So why the kidnapping and torture?"

Raery nodded, glancing down at the table a moment before her dark eyes connected with mine. "The kidnapping was to get time with you, a third party looking into the case. To see what you knew and help you understand we couldn't have committed these murders. As for what you call torture, the lights and the test help us know if you've been hexed by one of the Council. It's a simple spell but can have devastating effects on getting genuine answers from someone."

"I take it I passed then?"

"For sure. The bright light beam is the biggest tester. If a person has been hexed, they won't move their head away from the light source."

"I get trying to test people, but the siren sound and then hitting me? I didn't need that."

Raery raised her hands in a calming manner and said, "I promise, my girls wouldn't do that unless you'd attacked them first. We've never had someone break through the cuffs and escape. It's good to know where we're vulnerable though."

I glanced down at my notebook, words and phrases written haphazardly along the page. I scanned the information again, trying to figure out what to ask next. Having plenty of time to interview someone didn't often happen in my line of work. Just like the interrogation of Stanley the other day, most of my questions went unanswered and it was a relief to be getting the real answers I needed.

"Okay, how many others were there in your initiation? Is that what Alina was doing? Trying to make it into the secret society and she got killed?"

"She was part of the running class that year, but the group working together had been more powerful than many of the classes before. Not as powerful as your mother and I with our pledge class, but they began experimenting with magic."

I tried to picture my mother, entering a secret society and learning about more powerful types of magic. I would have experimented, given the chance.

"Becoming a part of the order means that after several tests, the bruja is pure of heart when it comes to dealing with the darker stuff."

I was floored. "What do you mean, 'pure of heart'? I thought secret societies did things to influence politics for their good."

"That is where we differ from the regular societies. We are

the holders and protectors of the greatest and darkest magic possible."

What dark magic was she talking about? Was the Codex considered great and dark magic?

My eyes caught on the word Mary and a thought popped into my mind. "Does Mary still have access to everything in the bruja lands? She said something about being kicked out of the coven if she missed one of the council meetings."

I sat with my pen poised over my notebook, waiting for anything Raery might know to guide me from here. I suspected the Grand Mistress and Mary could still work together on things. But why would Mary kill her own daughter?

Raery's eyes narrowed. "Then the woman lied right to your face. She is one of the biggest supporters of the Council. And she wouldn't still live in bruja lands if they had thrown her out of the coven."

Irritation burned in my chest. I hated being lied to, and it seemed like Crescent City was the place of the ultimate secrets.

"Okay, so what spell is it the killer is using?"

"It's called tirant magía. It's considered dark magic."

"And why wasn't this figured out at the time of Alina's death?" It sounded blunt, like I was blaming the head of a secret society for the unsolved murder of a teenage girl, but I needed to know what obstacles I was facing.

Raery stopped, looking as though she was trying to find the words. "There was a lot of name calling, accusations thrown at the Black Order. To the point where we had to stop meeting for several months because of the threat that someone might find us and start killing more of our members."

Sounded something like the Salem Witch Trials.

"Whatever they say about us, know we are doing every-thing we can to keep the evil trapped."

"Wait, what evil?"

Raery's lifted her hand to the doorknob. "There isn't time to go over it, but years ago, one of the most powerful bruja was trapped in a secure location in the hopes of saving our race. She'd completed a spell that made her unkillable, which is why she was trapped."

This was all new information. I made a note to investigate it in my mother's journals. "I've only heard about the society from Sage. Why do you think the Council blames you for these killings?"

Sage popped up as my third suspect, but I was only half-serious about her on my list. The hot and cold persona made it difficult to get a good read on her, and I wondered if she could have done all this. She'd given me some positive help, but had it been for an ulterior motive? Had she been faking about being against the Grand Mistress while really trying to get information to feed to the older woman?

"You saw Alina's friends in the sanitorium, right?"

I nodded, not sure how it connected with the Black Order being framed for murder by the head council.

"They've blamed us for everything that's happened since the last time we saw your mother."

I nodded, hoping she would keep going. "When was that?"

"The night before she was murdered."

THIRTY-ONE

Something in me exploded, and I strode forward, standing right in front of the woman. I wished I didn't have to look up into her face.

"What are you saying? Did you have anything to do with my mother's murder?" I had to clench and unclench my fists at my side, hoping to get answers before I started hitting things.

"I am your mother's best friend, Claire. I always sided with her." She took the picture from her pocket and held it up to my face again, using her long pointer finger to tap at the woman on the other side of my mom from Adelaide. She looked close, but then again, all four of them were sitting next to each other, smiles bright for the camera.

We'd been over the relationship, talked about the purpose of the Order being to protect the other coven members from dark magic, which led me back to the Codex and its whereabouts.

"Where is the Codex now?" I asked, curious about Raery's answer.

"We're hoping you have an idea about that."

I shook my head, giving them the same expression I'd given to Lee Vance back at the precinct. "I have no idea. I have a storage shed full of things to look through."

"You haven't found it in the cottage?"

I think my jaw hit the floor. "You know about that?" I breathed out. But then again, if the Grand Mistress and Mary had been on the outs with my mother, who better to keep her things safe than the one woman who'd been with her through the big stuff.

"We sealed up all her things and anything important to the coven once we took the Codex."

"I'm grateful for it, but why?" I asked, trying to put together the reasoning to lock up her things, especially if the Council didn't know about them.

"There are people within the Council, Beckett. People who would take away every right the bruja has."

"Not to burst your bubble, but life here looks like shit. How can you all live with so many rules?"

A loud knock came at the door, sending Raery from the demeanor of chatting over coffee to shoulders back and chin up as if preparing to enter battle.

"Come in," Raery said.

Sloan walked in, giving me a small smile before addressing Raery. "There's been another body." I should've known she would be here, since she'd been the one to show me the cottage.

"It won't be like this forever," Raery said, her voice tinged with weariness as she turned her attention back to me and stood. "Which is why we need to figure out who murdered Alina and Flora, before they murder again."

"True. Do you have evidence for who is killing the witches and shifters?"

The room went silent. Not the thing I wanted them to do now that I'd slowly gotten more information.

"What about Sage?" I said, trying to bait them. I had an inkling she was bugged about something, but I wasn't sure what, or to the lengths she would go to find out information.

"Sage is just the right-hand bitch to the Grand Mistress. It was Adelaide who orchestrated the whole thing."

"Alina's pledge group gave me five things. A piece of fabric, a coin, a half button, a piece of glass, and two sticks. Any idea what it could mean?"

Sloan nodded. "I was just looking this over today and thought it sounded familiar. It's a spell that takes a few random items and binds them. Maybe they were all bound to keep from talking or moving."

"They can stand," I said, reflecting over the disturbing sight it was to see all five girls posed the same in their cells. "What would be the purpose of making it so they can't function normally?"

"It makes it a lot harder to find the killer," Raery said. "Look at how long it's taken us to get to this point."

"The sun's up," someone said from outside the door and I glanced at them, wondering what it had to do with our conversation.

Raery stared at me. "How much longer do you have to solve the case?"

I tried to think of how long I'd been here already and I said, "The Grand Mistress originally said two weeks, but I would guess about three or four days left. If everyone is dying, I need a solid suspect by tonight."

Raery stood and said, "I'm sorry to cut the history lesson short, but we need your help. And the best way to do that is by sending you back to the Council to find the killer."

"Sure, anything," I said, hoping I hadn't agreed to something that would get me fired from my job. But because my mother had led these people made me want to do anything so I could learn more.

"They will accuse us of these murders, if they haven't already. Each one of the bruja who've been killed are part of this Order and we never betray our own."

I started at that. "Alina and Flora were part of the Order?" When she nodded, I continued. "What about the shifters killed over the past few weeks?"

Her expression was perplexed, and she frowned. "I'm not sure what happened outside the bruja lands. Maybe practice? But the spell used for the killings is very intense and needs exceptional power."

I pulled out my notebook, disappointed at having to wait longer for answers about my mother's life. But in order to save more bodies from a six-foot grave, I needed to get back into detective mode.

"You said you never betray your own. Why haven't you rescued Alina's friends from the sanitorium? And Flora's friends who've gone missing. Where are they?" The words poured out of me, and I took in several deep breaths, preparing myself for what would be important for the case at hand.

"We're doing our best to get everything back in balance. Rescuing the girls from the sanitorium would alert the Council to our whereabouts, and we aren't in a place where we can take on the entire coven, nor do we want to. But to get to those girls, we need to be absolved of any killings, which we didn't commit."

Another knock sounded and the girl from the other room, Hannah, appeared. "They found a second body. On the other side of the dining hall."

Raery turned to me. "I'm sorry, Claire. We need to get you back there. Solve this, will you?"

I swallowed hard, feeling the weight of the request press down on me. "I'll do what I can."

Two hooded figures walked into the room, one holding a burlap sack. She moved with stealth and stuck it over my head, while the other trapped my hands with the familiar cuffs.

"This is just procedure, Claire. The Council knows you've been kidnapped for the past three days." I felt a hand on my shoulder, the slight squeeze letting me know it was Raery.

That wasn't as specific as I'd have liked, but I knew I'd get answers from her when the crisis had been taken care of.

And with that, I felt a pinch in my arm, a weightless sleep pulling at me. And again, everything went black.

THIRTY-TWO

My phone rang loudly against my ear. I woke up, seeing Heath's name on the screen.

"Heath," I said, sitting up. I blinked a few times, but I was back in the room Sage had showed me to however many days ago. "Are you okay?"

"What the hell, Beckett? Am I okay? Where have you been? We've been searching for three days. Sage called saying you'd been kidnapped and we've scoured the coven, even sending my people over to the shifter lands to see if they could get your scent at all." His voice conveyed pure frustration and I couldn't help but smile.

"I'm fine. Just got a massive headache right now." I rubbed at the back of my head, feeling a bump along the bottom of my skull. There was no mark where I'd felt the pinch on my arm yesterday. I'd thought someone had drugged me to get out of there, but it turned out I'd been hit on the head again. They were bruja. Couldn't they have come up with a better way to keep me from knowing the route to their secret hideout?

Heath groaned. "Is it because of the bruja? Does that make

you have headaches? Because every time you've complained about one, it's because you've been around them for too long."

"This headache isn't like those ones, and I haven't complained. I think I've been pretty strong about them, considering they bring me to my knees."

"Where are you?"

"In the dorm where Sage brought me."

I thought I heard a sigh of relief. "All hell broke loose. I suggest coming out to help me with the damage before I come in and drag you out."

"I'd like to see you try," I muttered, my brain coming up with the sounds of him pounding down my door.

"What was it?"

"Nothing. I'll be right out."

I hung up the phone, realizing they had changed me back into my clothes. It would have been easy to convince myself the meeting with the Black Order had all been a dream, except I had a large dark spot staining my shirt. Dried blood from my nose. Touching my nose softly, I smiled when I didn't feel a break. Thank you, shifter abilities.

With my phone in my back pocket, I slipped my feet into my boots, more grateful for them than I ever thought I would be. I gathered the small pieces the girls had given me from the desk and slipped them into an inner pocket of my leather jacket.

If they were a binding spell, there had to be a way to break it.

I wasn't coming back to this room if I had any say. We were going to find a killer tonight, and I was going to sleep in my own bed. Because another body dead was too many we'd already lost to this murderer.

THIRTY-THREE

The sky was bright overhead, and I had to squint, blinking rapidly for several seconds so my eyes could adjust.

Something hit me in the gut, knocking the wind out of me. I glanced down, trying to catch my breath and saw a black duffle bag.

"That's for causing enough trouble to call out the protector cavalry," Heath said, his voice more of a snarl.

With my lungs functioning correctly again, I picked up the duffle bag and slung it over my shoulder. "You missed me, huh?"

"When the mutt I'm supposed to be protecting goes MIA for three days, I go through all the emotions." He bared his teeth, but the look in his eyes didn't instill fear in me, more like it showed the relief running through him.

I glared at him. "I'm not a dog, you said so yourself. So, don't ever, ever," I said, stepping closer to him, "call me a mutt again."

It was one thing to call myself that, but coming from his

angry countenance, it sounded like the lowest thing that could inhabit the earth.

"Where the hell were you?" he asked, our faces closer than they'd ever been. I could feel his hot breath on my face and I might have dropped my gaze to his lips a few times.

"Doing my damn job, okay?"

"Detective Beckett," Sage said, hurrying up to the side of us. I took a large step back, focusing my attention on her as she approached. "You're alive. I was sure the Black Order had found you and continued their streak of killing here."

I turned my body so it was parallel with hers. Interesting that she'd make such a quick assumption. What did she know, and what was her angle?

"What would make you think the Black Order had done something like this? Wasn't it you who told me they'd disbanded their organization?" My teeth ground together. I wasn't in the mood to deal with another liar.

She went slack-jawed, as though I'd just slapped her with my words. "It's not like that. I promise. The Grand Mistress believes the Black Order is still meeting despite the trouble they've caused our coven."

"You're on Eleanor's side then, huh?"

The woman's lips sputtered, trying to come up with some excuse but failing. I glanced at Heath instead and said, "Do you by chance come with anything we can use to tie her up?"

The space between his eyebrows disappeared, and he grinned widely. "Aren't you supposed to carry them around as a cop? Hell, the last suspect you had to hold was tied with sheets."

"What can I say? I'm good at improvising." My lips suddenly felt dry, and I had to look away. Joking with Heath would have to wait for another time.

Sage took off, heading toward the Council building.

"Are you going to just let her go?" Heath said, turning.

"That's what you're for. I'm just giving her a head start to test your speed, since we didn't see it at the Shifter Games finale, right?"

Heath groaned and sprinted after her, running a hell of a lot faster than my legs could take me. Was I going to be cursed with reptile speed now? I thought snakes could move quickly, but a salamander? It definitely wasn't a cheetah.

By the time I caught up to the two of them, I was breathing a lot harder than normal. The slight ache in my forehead burned, and I was dizzy. Probably from the dozen times I'd been hit on the head in the Black Order compound, wherever it was.

"Sage, you're under arrest on behalf of the Crescent City PPD for the murders of Alina Young, Flora Cyan, and several others we will name during your trial."

"I didn't kill them, I swear." She was on her knees, her hands raised. Her eyes had to be the size of golf balls, terror causing her body to shake.

I frowned. "You expect me to believe you after all the acting and lying you've done? No, you'll be heading back into town with the Mayor. We've got just the cell for you. It doesn't have much of a view, but after killing this many people, I would think you'll get the death penalty soon."

Adrenaline pumped through me, the words spilling out faster than my thoughts could catch up with.

"I'll help you solve this. It wasn't me who killed those people." The quiver in her voice caused me a slight hesitation. Heath growled behind her and I glanced over at him. He said nothing, but I knew he would want to hear all the plausible evidence.

Shaking my head, I said, "Again, I don't believe you."

"There's a letter in my right front pocket. Just let me pull it out and I'll show you."

"I don't care about any letters. You could have forged it to deny any involvement."

Heath held one hand behind her back and let the other one go. "She has the right to prove innocence, Beckett. Just because your judgment is clouded doesn't mean the rules change."

Fury burst through me and if I could shoot fire out of my eyes, he would be a pile of ash right now.

Sage pulled out a paper and handed it to me. "They placed this under the door to my apartment the morning you showed up for the hearing."

I opened the paper, surprised the thick parchment had even fit into the pocket of her skinny jeans.

Delay the detective as long as possible. Rewards will come.

"That's it? That's the note, and you believed it? I hope you know tampering with an ongoing case is a federal offense." I shook my head, stopping quickly when it produced the searing headache. "What could you possibly hope to gain from enforcing something so vague?"

Sage's gaze turned to the ground and her lower lip trembled. Damn, she was the best actor I'd ever seen.

"I'm trying to get out of the coven. You've seen the living conditions here. I want no part of it. If I have to do a little detouring to earn money to leave, I will."

"I think she's telling the truth, Beckett. She might be a leech, but she didn't kill the victims."

"Whose side are you on, Mayor?"

He rolled his eyes, his large hand still wrapped around Sage's bicep, holding her in place.

"If you didn't kill these girls, who did?" I kept my eyes locked onto hers, making sure she knew how serious I was about this. "If you want to be let go, you better start giving some answers to redeem yourself."

"I told you the truth earlier, about the Grand Mistress making plans she wasn't sharing with the rest of the Council. Whatever she's planning might be connected to the murders."

It wasn't a lot, but I'd been meaning to pay the Grand Mistress a visit, anyway.

I motioned to Heath. "Bring her along. Maybe we can use her as leverage to get what we need in the answer department."

THIRTY-FOUR

Answers were like lost fossils in this place. Everything seemed old but their secrets were all buried deep.

We'd made it to the council building, and I'd told Heath to stay outside with Sage for a few minutes. I didn't want to play all my cards at once and seeing if Adelaide would rat out Sage as the killer without her there would help me.

"Ah, Detective Beckett," the Grand Mistress said as we walked through the doors of the Council building. Sage had guided us toward her chambers and offices, which helped since this seemed like some big maze of hallways. "Any progress on the case? We have two more bodies with similar causes of death."

"Where were you during each murder?" I didn't bother to get my notebook out, knowing the facts of today. Had she been mad enough to kill so many victims because they didn't include her into the Black Order? But what about the shifters? Would she have stooped to doing something so vile and the chance it could get her caught?

"I've been dealing with coven business during each event,"

the Grand Mistress stated, licking her lips as though she'd just tasted something bitter. "I am charged with protecting this coven and wouldn't do anything to hurt its members. We are waging a war against evil, and I need as many warriors on my side as possible. Killing some of the most powerful bruja would be a bad way to direct an army."

"I'll need a list of alibis for your whereabouts during each murder." I didn't trust these women and wondered how a coven of however many bruja had lasted this long with her as the Grand Mistress and Sage the Snake as her right hand.

"What about Mary?" I studied the woman's face, looking for any slight change of emotion.

"What about Mary? There are at least a hundred Marys in my coven. You'll have to be more specific."

This woman was getting on my nerves. What had my mother seen in her as a friend? Then again, when I'd first met Tori, I wasn't the easiest to get along with. And many years had passed since my mom and Adelaide had been friends.

I blew out a breath, trying to keep my composure and not blow up at her ridiculous evasions. "Mary Michaels. You were friends with her growing up, correct?" When she nodded slowly, I knew I'd thrown her off-guard. "Do you think she'd commit these murders? I mean, from what I've learned from several sources, they had left the two of you out of pledging for the Black Order. Hate is a powerful motive."

The Grand Mistress looked like I'd thrown her off-kilter. She'd been so composed before, and now she might blow over with a light breeze. How had she been the same age as my mother? Did the use of so much magic cause a bruja to age faster?

"Mary and I were both bitter we hadn't been invited to pledge to the secret society, but we have never thought of hurting people because of it. Why would we after getting just about everything we want?"

I narrowed my eyes, not following her explanation. "What do you mean, 'Everything you want'?"

She waved her arms around the room. "This is what I've always wanted. To show the coven I might not have been accepted as a teenager for some damn secret society but I could rise and rule the whole of it."

Mary's face and small house came to mind. "And Mary?"

"She got the family she always wanted. Her husband is one of the head warlocks on the Council and the amount of power given to their children was all she'd dreamed."

"Except she never stopped talking about that damn Order." The voice was labored, and it took a few moments to locate the direction from which it had come. From the shadows stumbled Sage, her hands pressed against her abdomen, blood gushing out like a waterfall.

My first thought was to find somewhere to throw up, but it would have to wait. She was in trouble and I needed to help.

Sage stumbled to the ground, her head slamming against the concrete floor. She blinked a few times and exhaled.

I knelt beside her. "What happened, Sage? Where is Heath? Why isn't he protecting you?"

"Cin-dy." It was all she could get out.

"Cindy Michaels? Or Young," I said, trying to understand what that meant. Was she trying to signal Cindy was the next person to be killed?

And then my mind focused. Cindy was the killer.

Sage's breathing turned shallow and her heartbeat was almost gone. "Is there a spell to heal her? Put blood back inside her?"

The Grand Mistress nodded. "I don't know if it will work at this stage. She's already lost so much blood."

There was only one hole in her chest, and as I inspected her chest cavity, I saw her heart dissolve, until there was nothing left.

"Do what you can," I said to the Grand Mistress, pushing to my feet. I didn't hold out much hope for the first assistant, knowing if we couldn't get the heart back, and fast, she wouldn't survive much longer.

I ran out into the hallway, searching for any sign of Heath. It wasn't like him to abandon his post, especially when a psycho killer was nearby. How had Sage gotten away from him anyway?

"Heath! Heath!" I called, running down the hallways. There was no sign of anyone else in the building. It took a few tries, but I made my way out into the cool night, hearing something skid along the ground to my left.

Cindy stood poised with her hands outstretched, both of them covered in dark red blood. A small brown sack was at her feet, blood covering a section as well. Is that where Sage's heart was? I cringed, not wanting to think about a beating organ stuck into a dirty bag.

Across from her, Heath sat up, looking groggy from whatever she'd done to him. She spat out several words, the frustration tightening up her features as whatever she'd tried to do hadn't worked.

"You're supposed to die, just like the other dirty shifters."

"Cindy?" Doing my best to cover up the shock, I said, "You killed these people? You killed your own sister?"

A slow smile spread across her face. "Why so surprised? She deserved what was coming to her. Our mother bemoaned the fact she hadn't been chosen for the Black Order at least once a day for our entire lives. Her two so-called friends, one even *family*, had taken it away."

My heart sped up, thudding in my ears and making it more

difficult to hear what she was saying. At least we were getting a full confession, even if I was still reeling from how wrong I'd been about the suspect. Again.

"Why kill Alina?" I asked, taking a couple of steps forward, hoping I could delay any more spells by keeping up a conversation.

"Because she got invited to the Order and she accepted it. How could she do that? How could she be so unfeeling about what our mother had been through for so long?" Cindy's eyes flashed and she repositioned her body to parallel mine, her hands still outstretched.

Oh shit. I hadn't prepared for this.

I tried to find anything around me that could act as a shield, but tree branches wouldn't help with that.

"Spoiled shit. They'd given her everything because she was supposedly a gifted bruja. Not so gifted after a little hex, now was she?" The anger and frustration on Cindy's face was familiar, and I could understand how being overlooked for so long would cause her to act, but to kill? That was a bit extreme.

"How did you find out about her acceptance to the Black Order?"

Cindy sneered, tipping her chin up. "When a sister who shares everything with you suddenly pretends you no longer exist, it's easy to put the pieces together. It's exactly what my mother's cousin did to her."

I swallowed, trying to calm my nervous system at the accusation. She didn't know I was connected to her mother's cousin, or that in some strange way, I was related to this crazy girl. Maybe Raery was right. I wasn't ready to meet anyone else in the Michaels clan.

"And the others?" I stared at her for several seconds, and when she didn't answer, I continued. "What about the shifters and animals you killed? And what about Flora?"

Cindy gave me a smile that sent chills running up my spine. "Collateral damage. Flora for leaving her friends to be trapped without a second thought."

"Where are they, Cindy? Did you trap them?" My stomach clenched. There'd already been too much bloodshed. We didn't need more young bruja killed, no matter how strange this society was.

"I haven't seen the friends, no," Cindy said, raising a finger up and watching the blood wrap around it. Her eyes were wide with excitement and I wondered whether this was better or worse than my dealings with the vampires a few weeks ago.

I gulped, trying to regain my composure. "What about Alina's friends? What happened there? Did you torture them?"

The smile reappeared, stretching even further than before. "So many questions, Detective. I might've cast a spell over them. It was one they'd been practicing in their little group. The one they'd found that no one was supposed to know about."

"Were you friends with Flora?" I asked, a few things clicking into place. The hate of Alina had boiled up when she'd been accepted into the Black Order. And it sounded like Flora was part of this year's initiation class, but hadn't gone because she was sick.

Cindy spat on the ground. "Best friends. But what did she do? She had to stop talking to me because I wasn't part of her special group. What kind of society is it that tears friends apart?"

"What kind of friend kills her sister and best friend out of spite?" I couldn't control the bite in my words, nor the level at which they came out.

"One who has nothing left to lose," Cindy said, stretching her hands out and chanting some words that didn't ring true to me. The way her last few words broke reminded me of the *tvary* I'd seen. Heartbroken.

"Let me have the heart," I said, stretching an arm toward the bag. I wasn't prepared for a hex and didn't have any idea how to combat it.

"Give you the heart of a traitor?" Cindy cackled, sounding like she'd lost her mind. Then again, she'd killed several people and shifters. "So you can put her back together and everyone pretends like this never happened? She's the one who wanted to leave us, to escape our family for her own life. As you can see, I don't take well to betrayal."

I had little time to dwell on it as she moved her hand to the side, aiming at me. A burning sensation started in my chest, and it felt like someone had clamped their hands around my lungs, making it impossible to breathe.

"Beckett," Heath said, charging forward. He was limping, barely putting weight on his right leg.

"You can't save her," Cindy said, laughing. "I'll just finish you all off."

She jerked her hand back, as if trying to pull out my inner organs. But the burning sensation subsided and I opened my hands, chanting the words I used to close up the cottage every time. It had been a last second idea, and I was willing to try anything to ward off the attack.

Cindy's hands smoked and a bolt of electricity shot out of my hands, incapacitating her on the ground.

I bent over, breathing in deeply with the exertion I'd used. My pointer finger was hot, like I'd just pressed it onto a stove burner. Was I manifesting my fire?

I jogged forward, looking for something yet again to help me tie up my murderer. A pair of handcuffs would've been great right now.

"I didn't foresee Cindy being the killer," the Grand

Mistress said from behind me. Her appearance was disheveled and her shoulders drooped, like she'd lost everything she thought she'd had. "I should have seen the signs."

"Didn't anyone question the family?" That was usually the first round of suspects, and we would've avoided all this.

The Grand Mistress nodded. "We questioned a lot, but all the leads seemed to dry up before we could find anything. What will you do with her?"

"She'll have to be prosecuted. She's now a legal adult and with a handful of murders on her hands. It doesn't look good."

Cindy's eyes opened and they blinked a weird shade of bluish/purple. I remembered something about that in the file Tork had shown me on my first case. It was something about a witch coming into her full powers. Was that normal for a teenager?

Her hands came up, and mine matched hers, one hand shooting out electricity while the other was consumed in a bright red and orange fire.

Cindy stood, her eyes only glowing brighter. Her lips continued to move, but the ward I'd chanted moments before kept them from entering, as if her hex was a ball bouncing off a building.

She deflected the electricity but took a few steps back, showing me I was winning. I twirled the fingers of flame and stepped forward, trying to throw it at her. The flames hit her in the chest and threw her back against a nearby tree.

And just as soon as my confidence rose, the piercing headache began.

THIRTY-FIVE

It was too hard to think about anything but the pain. The slicing through my forehead, and this time, back through my brain reminded me of someone chopping vegetables.

I couldn't hear anything, and opening my eyes made the pain even worse. How did I combat that? And where was it coming from?

"Beckett," Heath said, practically shouting in my ear for me to hear. He had one arm wrapped around my back near my waist, as if trying to hold me up somewhat.

I shook my head, wishing I could just pass out. Vomit stuck in my throat, but I held it back, not wanting to puke in front of a killer.

"Stick out your hand. I'll guide you. Do everything you can to manifest your powers." His hand grasped my wrist, pushing my arm to the left a few inches. "She's still down, but you've got to defend yourself. I can't get past whatever ward she has set up."

I was so tired. Exhaustion settled into my back and it was like all the energy had been drained out of me.

"Fight, Claire," he said, his voice tinged with a worry I didn't know he could feel. "You're a fighter. Push past the pain."

His words called up all the images of pain I'd gone through over the past year. Gunshot wound, my best friend's murder, a broken ankle and the trauma of seeing Lee Vance's face everywhere.

Taking in a deep breath, I let it out, clearing my mind. I pushed at the pain in my head, focused on breaking it apart before it consumed me. There was still a hint of it there, but at least I could function.

I blinked, my eyes finally able to see the surrounding dangers. Cindy stood up, charred clothing and flesh visible at the side of her abdomen.

"You bitch!" Cindy yelled, positioning her hands for the hex. "Why couldn't you just leave us alone? We don't need the help of filthy half-breeds here."

I straightened to a standing position and shot a burst of electricity at her, hitting her in the head and knocking her back. Before I could shoot another to make sure the killer stayed down, chanting at the side of me caught my attention.

The Grand Mistress was positioned like she was ready to strike and once she finished speaking, Cindy's body spasmed and then collapsed.

"Why did you do that?" I asked, my breathing coming in huge gasps.

"Because there is no coming back from that kind of evil, Detective."

Heath knelt next to the body, checking for a pulse. He shook his head and stood.

I turned back to the Grand Mistress, trying to decide if I needed to arrest her or not. But a strange sense of triumph hit me. At least one killer wouldn't be a problem for me in the future.

"If you'll keep this as quiet as possible, we'd appreciate it," the Grand Mistress said quietly. "Our coven has... suffered a lot over the past several years." This was the first time I'd seen this woman so humble.

I nodded. "We'll do what we can. But the victims' families deserve to know what happened."

"I understand. How did you survive her initial attack?"

It was hard to explain, but a flash of memory cropped up, although it wasn't from my perspective. I was sitting in the interrogation room at the Black Order compound. The eyes I was looking through seemed to be Sloan's and it was as if her brain was telling mine the shot they injected into my arm was some kind of spell blocker. I didn't know how extensive it would go, but I also didn't want to find out today.

"No idea."

The Grand Mistress picked up the small bag. "If you don't mind, Detective, I'm going to see if I can revive my assistant."

The inner debate was quick, but a person's life was on the line. Sure, she'd tried to double-cross me, but I didn't need that on my head.

I nodded, and the woman walked inside.

A lightheaded sensation hit me, and my legs gave out. I expected to land onto the dirt and grass below, but strong arms caught me, cradling me against his chest.

"Thanks for catching me," I said, unable to keep my eyes open. The smell of Heath was like all the comfort I'd been lacking over the past few days.

Right before I fell asleep, I thought I felt him kiss the top of my head and whisper, "Every time."

THIRTY-SIX

"We hope to honor the names of those killed in the recent attacks. Please take a moment of silence."

The crowd packed into the Shifter Stadium was even more than a few weeks before. At Heath's insistence to finish the Games but also to unite the packs and covens, he'd made sure to invite everyone in the paranormal sector of Crescent City.

Most groups, packs, and covens stayed within the same areas, rarely mixing, but maybe we'd made some progress in unification of the paranormal community.

Seconds ticked by and my gaze bounced around the crowd, recognizing the faces of Alina's friends, the ones I'd found in the sanatorium. To see them smiling and laughing, normal young women after all they'd gone through was something.

The counter curse had been found among Cindy's things, which she'd apparently taken from some old book of her mother's. She'd even planted all the pieces for the girls, making them think it was part of the Black Order initiation and when they touched the objects, the hex had taken root.

As for her method of killing, she cast the hex on the person at least an hour before it affected the victims. It allowed her to get as far away from the person or animal, which is why there had been no leads from her sister's death three years ago.

How a young girl could be filled with so much hatred seemed like a stretch for me, but again, anything was possible here in the paranormal world. And if she was trying to protect her own mother, some would go to lengths to avenge family.

Hell, I was on my own quest to do it, which made judging her that much harder. At least I wouldn't have to testify at a hearing for it.

"Let the finals of the Shifter Games begin."

"I'll be so glad when this is over," Stacia said, coming to my side. She sipped on a soda and watched the field.

I grinned, laughing about her attitude. "Tork driving you crazy?"

He'd been stretching and doing little drills inside the bullpen ever since we'd wrapped up the case a few days before.

"Yes," she said, rolling her eyes. "Why is it you guys have to compete like this to feel like they're worth anything?"

My eyes caught onto the massive form of Heath, watching as he turned into his wolf form. Something about that stirred the attraction to a whole new level. But nothing could compare to what I hoped wasn't a dream as he'd carried me from the Shadowmoon Coven lands.

"I'm not sure. But I know we can give them shit about it at any point." The two of us laughed, and it felt comfortable. I hadn't had a good girlfriend since Tori died, and I hadn't realized how much I'd missed talking to another woman. Nina had been a good resource for talking about basic things, but she was still in Boston.

"How are things with your sister?" Stacia asked, as if reading my thoughts.

I nodded. "Good, so far. I mean, Heath didn't let her know

they kidnapped me. Just said I'd had to go undercover for a few days. We've talked on the phone and to be honest, I'm hoping she gets the job in Boston. I'm not ready for her to know about all this just yet." I waved my hand around at the crowd.

"That isn't really your choice, though, is it?"

"True, but the longer she can go on believing the world is only so big, the easier it will be to protect her." It was funny to think of myself protecting her since I had the man-wolf nearby at all times.

The gun shot and the beasts lumbered off down the track. They took the turn much faster than normal humans, and they were soon sprinting past us.

"I might need a slow-motion camera on this one," I said, laughing.

"That's an idea. I don't think I saw Tork's feet touch the ground."

Three more laps and it came down to Tork and Heath in the lead. From our angle at the side of the track, I saw Tork was ahead by at least a step and wondered what would happen if Heath lost.

Was he a sore loser?

"Is this *the* race?" I asked Stacia.

"The one to decide the alpha? I think so." We both stood, waiting for those last few steps.

Tork was out ahead and then it was like everything turned to slow motion just for me, his stride much shorter than before as Heath's paw crossed the finish line first.

Did Tork just throw the race?

The crowd erupted with cheers and I stood there, stunned.

It took a while for us to get out to the guys, but Stacia was bouncing up and down at the fact Tork had taken second place. I didn't have the heart or the surety to tell her he'd let Heath take the lead.

They'd all transformed back into their human bodies and it was getting harder and harder to tear my eyes away from the beautifully sculpted abs and chest of Heath the Mayor. The man could be insufferable, but so damn hot.

"What did you think of that performance, Beckett," he asked, motioning to the track by pointing out with his lips.

From the look of joy on his face, he didn't know either. "It was pretty incredible," I said. "If you'd lost that one, would you no longer be the alpha?"

He nodded. "Usually that's how it works. Why?"

I shrugged. "Just curious."

"Great run, Tork," Heath said, looking over my shoulder as Tork and Stacia walked over. "Why don't we all go celebrate?"

"Yeah, sounds good," Tork said, smiling. "Let me get cleaned up first and we can head out."

Heath grabbed his bag and Stacia saw someone she knew, stepping away out of earshot.

"I saw that," I said, leaning into whisper.

Tork's eyes turned to focus on my face. "Saw what?"

"You threw the race."

Tork's hand flew over my mouth. He looked like he was about to die from lack of oxygen. "Don't say a word, ever. Heath is the real alpha here, and I'm not taking over his job."

"It might not mean much, but you just showed me a whole other side of the great Detective Tork."

"Just shut up and go make goo goo eyes with the man, will you? It would make all our lives easier. He could use a distraction again."

What did he mean by again? I'd never thought about Heath's past relationships, but Tork's comment stirred up a slight jealousy I needed to hide.

With a grimace, I shook my head. "Celebrating means a drink, not tonsil hockey, Tork."

He chuckled. "Could've fooled me. See you there, Beckett. Let's just hope we don't get another case in the next thirty minutes."

"Yeah, I think we could all use a good break."

And then my phone went off. Gonzalez showed up on my screen.

"Beckett," I said, answering it.

"Beckett, this is Gonzalez. We just found a body outside a warehouse. Better get down here and take a look."

"I'll be there in five."

So much for a night off. Justice was now on the menu.

THANKS FOR READING book 3 in the Claire Beckett series.

Things are starting to heat up in more ways than one. There's so much history there, if only someone would fess up and tell her about her past.

Exploring a bruja secret society was a fun adventure. And what is with these villains trying to take out their own kind?

A favorite of this series is book 4, which introduces a character Claire doesn't expect, and they're forced to work together. Go grab the Kiss of Fire now and happy reading!

ALSO BY MOLLY CHASE

Claire Beckett: Protector of Crescent City Series

Claire Beckett and the Transfer of Power

Claire Beckett and the Hunted Fortress of Blood

Claire Beckett and the Black Order

Claire Beckett and the Kiss of Fire

Claire Beckett and the Cursed Temple

Claire Beckett and the Forbidden Secret

Claire Beckett and the Seeker of Darkness

Novellas

Death Hath No Claim

Sign up for Molly's newsletter and learn when the next book will drop!

ABOUT THE AUTHOR

Molly Chase grew up reading in a lot of genres. She wrote her first fantasy in fourth grade for a book contest. It took her a while to come back to that, but with five kids, that can happen to a person.

She's a mother, a reader, writer, athlete, and lover of chocolate chip cookies. In her down time, she loves crime dramas and sappy chick flicks.